ALL IT TAKES IS ONE SHOT . . .

Slocum, holding his rifle ready all the time, walked toward the fallen man. He was pretty sure the man was incapacitated, if not already dead, but he would take no foolish chances. The rifle had fallen where it was out of the man's reach. He walked even closer. He could hear the man's gurgling breath. He stopped, still standing, and looked down into the man's face.

"I don't even know you," Slocum said. "Why'd you make me do this?"

"One . . . One . . ."

The dying man was having trouble forming words, but Slocum figured him out. "One Shot?" he said. "Aaron Parsons. He put you up to this."

The man nodded slightly. Slocum dropped to one knee. He felt in Trump's shirt pocket and found a hundred dollars in wadded bills. He held it in front of the man's face.

"This what he paid you?" he asked.

He nodded again, weakly.

"Was it worth dying for?" Slocum asked. "You sold yourself too cheap, boy."

But there was no answer as the man's head rolled to one side. Slocum stood up, tucked the hundred into his own pocket, and turned to walk back to his horse . . .

DON'T MISS THESE
ALL-ACTION WESTERN SERIES
FROM THE BERKLEY PUBLISHING GROUP

THE GUNSMITH by J. R. Roberts
Clint Adams was a legend among lawmen, outlaws, and ladies. They called him . . . the Gunsmith.

LONGARM by Tabor Evans
The popular long-running series about U.S. Deputy Marshal Long—his life, his loves, his fight for justice.

SLOCUM by Jake Logan
Today's longest-running action Western. John Slocum rides a deadly trail of hot blood and cold steel.

BUSHWHACKERS by B. J. Lanagan
An action-packed series by the creators of Longarm! The rousing adventures of the most brutal gang of cutthroats ever assembled—Quantrill's Raiders.

DIAMONDBACK by Guy Brewer
Dex Yancy is Diamondback, a southern gentleman turned con man when his brother cheats him out of the family fortune. Ladies love him. Gamblers hate him. But nobody pulls one over on Dex . . .

WILDGUN by Jack Hanson
Will Barlow's continuing search for his daughter, kidnapped by the Blackfeet Indians who slaughtered the rest of his family.

SLOCUM
AND THE HIRED GUN

J
JOVE BOOKS, NEW YORK

This is a work of fiction. Names, characters, places, and incidents are either the product of the author's imagination or are used fictitiously, and any resemblance to actual persons, living or dead, business establishments, events, or locales is entirely coincidental.

SLOCUM AND THE HIRED GUN

A Jove Book / published by arrangement with
the author

PRINTING HISTORY
Jove edition / June 2001

The Penguin Putnam Inc. World Wide Web site address is
www.penguinputnam.com

ISBN: 0-515-13064-8

A JOVE BOOK®
Jove Books are published by The Berkley Publishing Group,
a division of Penguin Putnam Inc.,
375 Hudson Street, New York, New York 10014.
JOVE and the "J" design
are trademarks belonging to Penguin Putnam Inc.

PRINTED IN THE UNITED STATES OF AMERICA

10 9 8 7 6 5 4 3 2 1

1

Slocum sat alone at a table in a dark corner of the Red Ass Saloon in Harleyville, sipping good Kentucky bourbon and smoking a cigar. He had spent a good many days on the trail before riding into Harleyville and spotting the sign out front with the crude picture of a red donkey painted on it. Slocum had been riding from somewhere to—somewhere. He did not know where. He was dry from the long and dusty trail. Even so, he had first gone to the stable at the end of the street to take care of his big Appaloosa. Next he had gone into the hotel across the street from the saloon and rented himself a room. Then he had taken a long, hot bath and finally dressed himself in clean clothes. Only after all that had he left the hotel and gone across the street and into the Red Ass. He was a stranger in Harleyville. In spite of his many travels, this was new territory to him.

Without being obvious about it, Slocum checked out the other people in the saloon. There weren't too many. Harleyville was a small place. A woman in floozy clothes stood at the bar, hugging against a cowboy who was buying the drinks. The man behind the bar was a big man, tough-looking, the kind who looked like he could handle any rowdies who might decide to try to break the place up after they'd had too many drinks for their own good. There were three more cowhands at the bar, and two tables in the place were surrounded by drinkers. At one table the men all looked like town men, storekeepers, and such. At the other, Slocum figured one man to be a ranch owner and his companions all hands who likely worked for him. It was like a hundred other saloons in a hundred other towns Slocum had been in, and that made it comfortable, even though he was a stranger.

Suddenly a shriek from above split the air like lightning, and all heads turned toward the staircase that led up to the second floor. A young woman came running through the upstairs hallway and out to the landing there at the top of the stairs. A man came right behind her. He reached for her and got a handful of robe. She pulled herself loose and started running down the stairs, but he was right behind her. Once more, he got hold of her flimsy clothing, and once again, she tore herself loose from his grasp.

The woman was barefoot and wearing only the flimsy robe. Now that it was torn, one breast was exposed. The man was dressed from the waist down. Down on the main floor, the woman hesitated a moment too long, and he grabbed her by the hair, jerking her back against him. "Come on, you bitch," he said. "You're going to do what I want to do." She squealed and cried out, "Let me go." Slocum watched with interest. No one in the room made a move to interfere. The girl struggled, and the man slapped her hard across the face. Still no one made a move.

Slocum heaved a heavy sigh. The last thing he wanted in this strange town was trouble, and clearly this was none of his business, but enough was enough. He stood up. "That's about enough of that shit, mister," he said, and his voice rang loud and clear. The man, still holding on to the woman, looked over in Slocum's direction. So did everyone else in the room. Incredulous, the bully, his face cold and hard, said, "Are you talking to me?"

"I'm talking to you," Slocum said. "Turn her loose."

The man slung the woman away, knocking her back against the bar. He took a couple of bold steps toward Slocum. "I ain't wearing a gun," he said. "I was prepared for a different kind of play." Slocum unbuckled his gun belt and laid it on the table beside his drink. "This situation don't really call for gunplay," he said. He was alert to the others in the room. This bully could easily have friends among them. Still, no one moved. They all watched carefully though. Slocum walked toward the bully.

The bully spit on his hands and made them into fists. Then he held them out ready to fight. Raising his own fists, Slocum moved in close, then suddenly gave a swift kick to the bully's balls. The man roared in pain and surprise and doubled over. His face turned green. Slocum whopped him a good one to the side of the head with a right hand fist, and the bully dropped hard to the floor. He was out cold. Slocum turned and headed back for his drink. The woman stared at the lump of bully on the floor in disbelief. Her mouth was agape, and her eyes were wide. Then she hurried after Slocum. He buckled on his gun belt and sat back down. She pulled out a chair and sat down beside him, not waiting for an invitation.

"When he wakes up, he'll kill me," she said. "After he's killed you."

"If he's coming after me first," Slocum said, "you got nothing to worry about."

"You don't know him," she said. "He's a bad one."

"He don't look so bad right now," said Slocum. "And I don't need to know him. I've known a hundred like him. Bullies are always cowards. They're afraid of a real fight."

"But you don't know him," she said. "He'll come up behind you. He'll shoot you in the back. Or hit you in the head from behind with an ax handle or something like that."

"Relax," said Slocum. "Have a drink." He waved an arm at the bartender, who picked up a glass and tossed it across the room. Slocum caught it with his right hand, put it on the table, and poured it full. Then he shoved it over in front of the woman. He looked at her then, really for the first time. She couldn't have been thirty years old. She was wearing plenty of makeup, but underneath it all, she had a nice face, big blue eyes, and full lips. Her hair, cropped just above her shoulders, was blond. She picked up the glass and took a healthy drink.

"That better?" he said.

"Yeah," she said.

"What's your name?" Slocum asked her.

"Felicia," she said. "Felicia Frick. Who are you?"

"The name's John Slocum," he said.

"What brings you to Harleyville?" Felicia asked him.

"Just passing through," said Slocum. "It seemed like a good place to stop and rest up for a few days. It's been a long trail."

"You a cowboy?" she asked him.

"I have been," he said. "Been a lot of other things, too."

They heard a moan from over by the bar, and they looked and saw the bully stirring there on the floor. He groaned and rolled over on his back. His hands went down to his crotch, and he wrinkled his face in pain. He groaned again, louder this time. Then he rolled back over on his belly and got himself slowly up to his knees. Carefully he stood up, leaning back against the bar. He took several deep breaths. Then he looked around the room until he spotted Slocum and Felicia sitting together at the table in the back. He looked over at the cowboy standing nearest him at the bar.

"Give me your goddamn gun, Randy," he said.

"No way," said Randy.

"Someone give me a fucking gun," the bully roared.

"Forget it," Slocum said. "It ain't worth dying over."

The bully ran for the stairs and mounted them in a few steps. In another moment he came back down, strapping on his gun belt. He was still bare-chested. Slocum stood up, ready to kill if need be. He hoped it wouldn't come to that. "There's still time to change your mind," he said. The bully's hand went for his gun, but before he could even clear leather, he found himself staring at Slocum's big Colt cocked and pointed at his chest. He stopped still and stared. His jaw was hanging. His own revolver was just halfway out of the holster. Slocum lowered the barrel of his Colt just a bit.

"I could shoot you right where I kicked you," he said,

and then he lifted it again, but this time higher than before, "or I could blow your brains out. Or you could just turn loose of that gun and walk on out of here, and we could both forget the whole damn thing. It's your choice, mister. I don't give a shit one way or the other."

The bully dropped his gun back down into the holster, turned, and hurried out of the Red Ass through the front batwing doors. Swinging back and forth, they clattered and their hinges squeaked. Slocum put away his Colt and sat back down. He picked up his glass and took a sip. Then he lifted the burning cigar from the ashtray and puffed on it. Felicia looked at him with wonder. "No one's ever done that around here before," she said.

"Done what?" Slocum asked her.

"Buffaloed Toughnut like that," she said.

"Is that what he's called?" said Slocum. "Toughnut?"

"Toughnut Timmons," she said.

"Well," said Slocum, "his nuts ain't so tough after all, are they?"

Felicia laughed at that. *She's a pretty girl*, Slocum thought, *especially when she laughs*.

"Where you staying, John Slocum?" she said.

"Across the street," said Slocum.

"It's a nice-enough place," she said.

Just then, the man Slocum had figured for a rancher stood up from his place at the other table. He turned and looked at Slocum, then walked toward him, doffing his hat. Getting close, he gave Felicia a curt nod. Then he held a hand out toward Slocum.

"I'm Parley Young," he said. "That was quite a display you made with ole Toughnut there."

"Well, I didn't see anyone else making a move," Slocum said.

Young dropped his hand since Slocum hadn't bothered to take it, and he gave a shrug. "It didn't seem to be any of our business," he said.

"Whenever I see a man bullying a woman," said Slocum, "I make it my business. That's the way they raise men where I come from."

"And where might that be?" Young asked.

Slocum shrugged. "I come from a lot of places," he said.

Young gave Felicia a look, and Slocum read more than a little disgust in it. He had an idea what Young was thinking. "Yeah, well," Young said, "likely you're right about that. Anyhow, Toughnut's had that coming to him for a long time now. You, uh, just passing through, or might you be looking for work?"

"I'm passing through," Slocum said.

"Well," said Young, "if you change your mind and decide to stick around, I have a big spread just out of town to the east. I might could use you. If you're looking for a job, ride on out in the morning. We'll have ourselves a talk."

"What makes you think I can handle cows?" Slocum said.

"Did I say anything about cows?" said Young, and he grinned. Slocum made no answer. He sat and watched as Young turned and walked back over to the table where his own drinking companions waited and sat down again.

"You could do a whole lot worse," Felicia said in a low voice. "He's one of the two biggest men in the territory."

"Oh yeah?" Slocum said. He drained his glass and poured some more whiskey in it. "Who's the other one?"

"The other one's Carl Jimson," Felicia said. "His place is out west. You might say that Jimson and Young are rivals."

"And little ole Harleyville's stuck right here between the two of them," Slocum said.

"Yeah," said Felicia. "That's right."

"Is there trouble between the two of them?" Slocum asked.

"Well, not really," she said. "Not yet."

"That sounds like there's liable to be," said Slocum, "just any time. I might not have picked the best place for a rest after all."

What Felicia had just told him about the two rival ranchers, he thought, would explain Young's offer of a job when all he had seen of Slocum was his quick tangle with Tough-

nut. He wasn't looking for cowhands. He was looking for
fighters. He was anticipating trouble. Maybe he was even
planning on starting it. Well, Slocum wanted none of someone else's trouble. He wanted a couple of days rest. That
was all. He'd had nothing more than that in mind when he
stopped in Harleyville, and he hadn't seen anything yet to
change his mind.

"I'm not looking for work," he said.

He picked up the bottle and poured himself and Felicia
another drink. Just then Toughnut stepped back through the
batwing doors, his revolver already in his hand, already
cocked. He brought it up level fast and snapped off a shot
in the general direction of Slocum. It smashed the bottle on
the table, showering Slocum and Felicia with bits of glass
and sprays of whiskey. Slocum stood quickly, flipping the
table up for a shield for himself and the woman. She
dropped down behind it. He stood and pulled his Colt,
thumbing back the hammer at the same time. As he brought
it level, he pulled the trigger, sending a bullet smashing
into Toughnut's left shoulder. It was a bad shot. He'd meant
to kill the man.

Toughnut howled in pain and anger and snapped off another shot, but it went wild. Slocum fired again, this time
more carefully. This time the bullet hit its mark, tearing
into Toughnut's chest and heart. The bully jerked and trembled and fell back through the batwings. He landed on the
board sidewalk and lay stiff and still, his feet sticking
through the doorway into the Red Ass Saloon. Slocum
walked over to the door. He kicked one of the feet and got
no reaction. He hadn't expected one. He was pretty sure
that the man was dead. He stepped out onto the sidewalk
and gave the body a nudge.

Sure of the results of his second shot, he holstered his
Colt and went back inside. He walked over to the upturned
table and looked at Felicia, who was standing up by then.
"You okay?" he asked her.

"Yeah," she said. "Is he—"

"Deader'n hell," said Slocum. He grabbed the edge of

the tabletop and set it back upright. Then he looked over at the barkeep. "We'll need another bottle," he said, "and two more glasses."

The bartender reached under the counter and came up with the bottle and glasses and hurried on over to where Slocum and Felicia waited. He put them on the table. When Slocum reached into a pocket, the bartender said, "It's on the house this time, friend." Slocum gave him a curious look. "You did us a favor," the man said. Slocum shrugged and sat down. "Thanks," he said. He looked up at Felicia. "You going to sit down and have another one?" he asked her. She sat down. "Yeah," she said. "Thanks."

The batwings swung open wide and a middle-aged man wearing a black vest with a badge pinned on it stepped into the room. He looked around. "What happened here?" he demanded.

"I killed him," said Slocum.

The lawman walked over to Slocum's table. He gave Felicia a cursory nod.

"What happened?" he said.

Slocum gave him a brief version, and Parley Young stood up from his place and walked over to where the lawman stood. "I can vouch for his story, Merle," Young said. "I saw the whole thing. So did everyone else in here. Toughnut started it. He asked for what he got. He came in here with his gun already drawn and cocked and started shooting. Slocum here just defended himself is all. Likely he saved some of the rest of us in the process, the mood Toughnut was in."

Merle, the lawman, rubbed his chin and looked down at Slocum. "Slocum, huh?" he said. "Seems I've heard of a Slocum. A gunfighter, some say."

"Folks say a lot of things about me," said Slocum. "Saddle bum's probably the most accurate."

"What're you doing in Harleyville?" Merle asked.

"Just passing through," said Slocum. "Seems like I've already told that to everyone here. I've been on a long trail and got a longer one yet to ride. Stopped here for a bath and a little rest. That's all. I didn't go looking for this fight."

"All right," Merle said. "I believe you. I know what Toughnut was like, and Mr. Young here backs up your story. We'll write it down as self-defense and forget it. We're all better off with Toughnut out of the way anyhow. Ought to give you a medal. Guess you'll be riding on in the morning?"

"He might decide to stick around," Young said. "Might be he could get himself a job around here."

"Well," Merle said, but he didn't finish the thought. Instead he turned and walked back outside, stepping over the body in the doorway. Then Slocum saw the feet of Toughnut as the lawman dragged the body out of the way. Young looked down at Slocum. "No thanks?" he said.

"All you did was tell the truth," Slocum said. "You need thanks for that?"

Young grinned, shrugged, and turned away. He went back to his own table and companions. Felicia leaned in toward Slocum. "You ought to be nicer to Mr. Young," she said. "He's a powerful man in these parts."

"So you told me, but I can take care of myself," Slocum said. "And I don't need to lick the boots of no local rich man to do it."

"Well, from what I've seen tonight," Felicia said, "I believe it."

Slocum poured the glasses full again. "Say," he said, "is there someplace to get a good steak in this town?"

"This time of night," Felicia said, "there's only one place open where you can get something to eat. But you can get a pretty good steak there."

"Will you show me the way?" said Slocum. "You hungry?"

"Can you give me time to get dressed?" she said.

"Sure," he said. "I'll wait for you right here."

Felicia got up and hurried across the room and up the stairs. Slocum sipped his whiskey. He took another puff on his cigar. It was burned down short by this time. He put the butt in the ashtray. Parley Young stood up. "Well, boys," he said, "let's head on back to the ranch." The others stood up obediently. Slocum noticed that none of them hesitated. He was right. Young was their boss. As they headed for the door, Young turned back toward Slocum once more.

"If you change your mind," he said, "anyone in town can tell you how to find me." He left the Red Ass. Slocum finished his drink and poured another one. By the time he had finished that one, Felicia came back down the stairs. He was surprised at her fresh appearance. She had dressed, all right, but not in saloon gal frills. If he'd seen her out on the street, he might have taken her for a school marm or something. And she was good-looking. He stood up and walked to meet her.

"You look great," he said.

"Thank you," she said with a smile.

"Ready to go?" he asked.

"Yes," she said.

Slocum gave her an arm, and they walked out of the Red Ass together.

2

She led him down the street and around a dark corner to a small place called The Short Rib. One customer sat eating a steak. He glanced up and nodded at Felicia. "Hi, Carl," she said. The man she called Carl chewed a little more and swallowed hard. He daubed his lips with a white rag, and then said, "Howdy, Felicia."

"This here's John Slocum," Felicia said. "John, meet Carl Jimson."

Jimson raised his ass a bit from the chair and held out a hand. Slocum shook it. "Howdy," he said.

"Howdy, yourself," said Jimson. "You two want to sit down and join me?"

"We don't want to interrupt," Slocum said.

"Nonsense," said Jimson. "I hate to eat by myself. Sit down."

Slocum and Felicia each took a chair at the table with Jimson, and in another minute a fat, greasy man in a dirty apron stepped up to take their orders. Slocum ordered two of the best steak dinners the place had to offer, and the greasy man disappeared. "Slocum," said Jimson, setting the name in his brain, "what brings you to these parts?"

"Traveling through," Slocum said.

"It was you that was involved in that shooting a little while ago, wasn't it?" Jimson asked.

"I reckon it was at that," said Slocum. "Word travels fast in a small town."

"It was all Toughnut's doing," Felicia said. "He started it all, and—"

"Yeah, that's what I heard," said Jimson, interrupting. "Also heard that ole Parley Young offered you a job right after that."

"He did," said Slocum. "I turned him down."

"He'd have paid you good," Jimson said.

"Like I said, I'm just passing through," Slocum told him.

"Yeah," Jimson muttered, and he cut another bite of steak.

"From what I heard," Slocum said, "if I had taken his offer, I'd likely have wound up shooting at you or your hands."

Jimson looked up and stared Slocum in the eyes for a moment. "Likely you heard right," he said. "It'll come to that, eventually. Ain't no way around it."

"There's usually a way around it," Slocum said, "if both sides are reasonable."

"Yeah, well, you tell that to ole Parley," Jimson said. "I'm not trying to hire gunfighters. No offense."

"None taken," said Slocum.

The greasy man brought the steak dinners, and Slocum ordered coffee for himself and for Felicia. The man grumbled and walked away. He was back soon with the coffee. Slocum and Felicia were in the middle of their meals when Jimson finished his. He excused himself and got up to leave. "Pleased to make your acquaintance, Slocum," he said. "Good traveling to you."

"Thanks," Slocum said. "And good luck to you."

Jimson put his hat on and nodded to Felicia. "Good night, Miss Felicia," he said.

He went to the counter, paid the greasy man, and left.

"Well," Felicia said, "you've met the two richest men in the whole territory."

"This one seemed a bit more decent than the other one," Slocum said.

"Yeah," she said. "Carl's a nice man. It's Parley that's causing all the trouble. He's got plenty, but he wants it all. He'd like to run Carl out of business and out of the country. He wants Carl's ranch, I think."

"That's the way with some men," Slocum told her. "They get plenty and still they want more. They can't be satisfied."

"Yeah," she said. "That's Parley Young."

They finished eating with a little more small talk, and then they got up to leave. Slocum went to the counter to pay, but the greasy man said, "Mr. Jimson done paid for yours."

"Well, I'll be," Slocum said.

"I told you he was a nice man," said Felicia.

They walked outside together. The sun was low in the sky, and a slight chill was setting in for the night. "Which way you going?" Slocum asked Felicia. "I'll walk you there. Then I think I'll turn in for the night."

"Slocum?" Felicia said.

"Yeah?"

"You want some company for the night? I'm not working. I'm on my own time."

"In that case," said Slocum, "I'd be tickled to have some company."

They walked together to his room in the hotel on the second floor, and Slocum was thinking that the evening had turned out just about too good to be true. He had expected nothing more than a bath, a good meal, a few drinks, a good night's rest, and to hit the road again in the morning. He had gotten much more than that. Of course, he would just as soon not have had his two encounters with Tough-nut, but it had all happened, and he wasn't going to let it spoil his evening.

He let Felicia into the hotel room, then followed her. He struck a match and lit the oil lamp on the table, turning it down low. Then he made sure they were securely locked in the room. When he turned away from the door, he saw that Felicia was already beginning to shed her clothes, and he liked what he saw. Even so, he thought that there was something he ought to say.

"You know, you don't have to do this," he told her. "I did what I did over there in the saloon, because, well, because no one else was doing anything about it. It had to be done. That's all."

"I know," she said, "and that's why I want to do this. That and because I like you."

Slocum stepped over close and put a hand on each of her bare shoulders. Her breasts were also bare, round, and firm and bare and inviting. He pulled her close and kissed her on the mouth. Her kiss was warm and wet. She pulled away, and he let her go and began undressing himself. She finished wriggling out of her dress and stepped over to the bed to turn down the covers. Slocum sat down to pull off his boots. When he stood up again, she was there. She was naked, and she was lovely.

She reached for the waistband of his trousers and unfastened them, then shoved them down over his hips. She knelt as she pushed the trousers lower. Then with Felicia on her knees before him, his trousers down around his ankles, he stepped out of them. She looked up and found him more than ready for action. Her hands slid up his inner thighs until they reached his crotch, and there she fondled and teased him. Leaning forward, she shot out her tongue and gave a flicker and another. Then she opened her mouth wide and slurped, taking in all she could. She moved her head back and forth, causing incredible sensations to rush through Slocum's entire body.

Then she pulled away, stood, and took him by the hand to lead him over to the bed. She waited until he had crawled in, and then she climbed in on top of him. On her knees astraddle his body, she settled herself down until she felt him deep inside her. She sat still a moment, savoring the sensation, before she began to slowly rock her hips back and forth, sliding on his hips. She moaned with the pleasure of her ride.

Then she moved faster and even faster, until her moans became continuous and louder, and finally she stopped and dropped over forward pressing her own breasts against his chest. She kissed him hard and deep. At last she straightened herself up and started over again. Slocum marveled at her energy and her tremendous capacity for enjoyment. He counted at least seven times she'd had her full pleasure of him, and he knew that it had been more than that. Finally she lay on him again, panting. "I've had all I can stand," she said. "It's your turn."

He took hold of her with both arms and rolled them over until he was on top, and he began to pump, slowly at first, then harder and faster. He pounded against her over and over, driving deep until he felt the pressure built up to its greatest force, and suddenly he burst forth with a series of powerful eruptions, flooding her deep inside. He rolled off her, lay on his back, and breathed deeply. Soon, naked, side by side, they both slept.

They had breakfast together at the little place around the corner. The same man was there, and Slocum was sure he was wearing the same greasy apron. The coffee was good though, and the breakfast of steak and eggs was all right, too. Slocum ate his fill and drank all the coffee he wanted. He smoked a cigar, lingering for a while. At last, he decided it was time to go.

"Where are you headed?" Felicia asked him.

"I'm not sure," he said. "I just feel like it's time to move on."

She thought about the night before, not just about the pleasant part of it, but earlier when he had fought with and then killed a man. He had done it in her defense. "Yeah," she said, and there was a sadness in her sweet voice. "I guess you're right. I'm glad you stopped by though. I'm glad I got to know you, John Slocum."

He smiled at her and squeezed her hand. "It's been a pleasure, lady," he said.

He'd paid his bill at the hotel, and he had his blanket roll thrown over his shoulder. He stepped into the big open front door of the stable, but it was dark inside. He looked

around for the little man who had taken in his horse, but
he could see no one. "Hello," he called out. There was no
answer. "Hey! Anyone here?" He was ready to pay the bill
and ride on out of town. He called out again, and still he
received no answer. He decided to go ahead and saddle the
big Appaloosa. Perhaps the man would come in before he
was ready to ride. He took a step farther inside, moving
toward the stalls, when he felt something smash him across
the shoulder, and he pitched forward to the ground.

Before he could scramble to his feet, a big boot kicked
him hard in the side, and another kicked his other side. He
covered his head with his arms and took several more kicks.
Finally the kicking stopped, and he felt arms take hold of
him and pull him to his feet. Two men held him from behind, one on each arm. A third took hold of his hair from
behind and pulled his head back. A big man with an evil
grin and a scar across the right cheek stepped up close in
front of him.

"We get your attention, mister?" he asked.

"You got it," said Slocum.

The man drove a fist into Slocum's midsection.

"That's just to make sure," he said. "I heard you're pretty
tough. And slick with your six-gun. But you see, that don't
make no difference around here."

"I can see that," said Slocum. "What's this all about?
You friends of that Toughnut?"

"Toughnut didn't have no friends, stranger," said the
scarface. "And you ain't got no friends around here neither.
That means you ain't wanted around here. You was seen
last night having supper and jawing with Carl Jimson. If he
made you an offer, you ain't taking it. Or if you done took
it, you're going to ride out of here and not show up for
work. You had a good offer made to you, and you chose
to turn it down. So just get on your horse and ride on out
of here. Don't look back."

The scarface slugged Slocum across the face then. Then
again. First a right. Then a left. Then he drove a final right
into Slocum's gut. Slocum sagged, and the scarface said,
"Let him drop." The three men behind him turned loose

and Slocum fell forward. "Come on," said the scarface. He started walking out the big door, and the other three followed him, but the one bringing up the rear, hesitated, looked back at Slocum, turned, and gave him a final kick in the side. Slocum groaned and rolled over. He managed to raise his head to get a look at the four men as they walked away. He would remember them.

He rolled back over to his belly and painfully got himself up to his hands and knees. A sharp pain shot through his body, and he was sure that at least one rib was broken. He straightened himself up, gritting his teeth against the pain. There was a tooth knocked loose, too. He sat there on his knees, sucking in deep breaths, but each breath sent stabbing pains from his rib cage through his chest and back. Finally he pulled one foot out from under himself and planted it flat. He tried to stand, but the stabbing pain stopped him. He felt almost helpless. He put pressure on his foot again in an attempt to rise, but the pain almost caused him to cry out loud.

"John?" a sweet and concerned voice called, and he looked up toward the front door of the stable. Felicia was there. She squinted into the dark interior of the stable and saw him. She ran over to him and knelt there beside him. "John," she said, "what did they do to you?"

"Never mind that right now," he said. "Just help me stand up."

She let him put an arm around her shoulders, and together they stood, but the pain was nearly unbearable, and the last thing he remembered, the whole world turned black, and he was swirling.

He woke up in a strange bed. Slowly things came back to him. He remembered the beating in the stable, and he recalled that Felicia had come to his aid. More than that, he did not know. He looked around. He was in someone's home. It was a pleasant bedroom. He tried to sit up, but the pain in his sides prevented it. With a moan, he lay back again. Then he realized that he was undressed, and that someone had taped his ribs. Tightly. He had no idea where he was, but wherever it was, he couldn't get up and go anywhere anyhow, so he decided to try to sleep some more. Just then, the door opened and Felicia came walking into the room. She had a pleasant smile on her face.

"John, you're awake," she said. "Good. How do you feel?"

"Like I been stomped on," he said. "Which I was."

She walked over and took a chair beside the bed. "Can I get you anything?" she asked him. "Are you hungry?"

"No thanks," he said. "But tell me where I am."

"You're at Carl Jimson's ranch house," she said. "I didn't know what else to do."

"How'd you get me here?" he asked her.

"After those men left, Sully came back," she said.

"That the stableman?" Slocum asked.

"Yeah," she said. "Sully. I made him hook me up a wagon and help me get you in it. Then I drove you out here. I brought your horse and saddle, too. And your blanket roll. As soon as you're feeling up to it, you can ride on out of here without going back into town."

"I appreciate what you did," said Slocum, "but how did you know—"

"I saw you go in the stable," she said. "A little later I saw those four come out. I was afraid they'd done something—like what they did."

"Do you know those men?" he asked her.

"Yes," she said.

"My bet is that they work for Parley Young," he said.

"They do," she said.

"I got a good look at one of them," he said. "Scar-faced bastard. I might be able to spot the other three."

"John," she said, "just forget it. Ride clear of here. Don't look for any more trouble. You were lucky this time. The next time could be worse."

Before he could answer her, Carl Jimson walked into the room. "I thought I heard some talking in here," he said. "Glad to see you still alive, Slocum. You took a hell of a pounding."

"That I did. I'm obliged to you, Mr. Jimson," Slocum

said, "for allowing me to be brought in here like this."

"Least I could do. Seems to me it was my fault you got into this shape," Jimson said. "Them four was convincing you not to work for me. Wasn't they?"

"They did mention that," said Slocum. "Said someone had seen us eating together last night. Damn their hides. Hell, I was on my way out of town."

"I know that," said Jimson. "They wanted to make sure though. It's early, I know, but you reckon you could use a drink?"

He brought a bottle of bourbon out from behind his back.

"I sure could," Slocum said.

Felicia took the bottle from Jimson and poured Slocum a drink in a glass that was sitting on the table beside the bed. Slocum took the glass and tried awkwardly to drink from it. Felicia took it back and put it on the table. She looked at Jimson. "Give me a hand, Carl," she said. "Would you please?" Jimson walked to the other side of the bed, and he and Felicia together managed to get a grimacing Slocum up to a half-sitting position with pillows behind his back. Felicia handed him the glass again, and he drank.

"Thanks," he said. "Say, what's that scar-faced man's name?"

"Jerry Goodall," said Jimson. "He's Young's hatchet man."

"The other three?" Slocum asked.

Jimson looked questioningly at Felicia.

"There was Buck Snider," she said, "Jody Tallman, and Red Orwig."

"You're not thinking about going after them, are you?" Jimson asked.

"Well, not right away," said Slocum, "but I reckon I'll see them again one of these days. When I do, I'll remind them of this morning."

"Well, you stick right here till you're in good shape again," Jimson said. "You ain't in no shape to go riding off, much less taking on the likes of them four."

"I won't burden you for long," said Slocum. "I'll ride

out in the morning. But one of these days, I'll be back through here."

"Now, look here, Slocum," said Jimson, "I won't have you riding out of here tomorrow, nor anytime too soon. They got you stove up pretty bad. I won't have it said of me that I let a man in that shape ride away from my ranch. You'll stay on here. You got that?"

Slocum took another drink of whiskey.

"That's good whiskey, Mr. Jimson," he said. "All right, I'll stay, but I have a couple of conditions. Not that I'm in any shape to be laying down rules around here."

"What do you want, Slocum?" said Jimson.

"Soon as I'm able, I want to work off what I owe you."

"Fair enough," Jimson said. "You said a couple."

"I want Felicia to stay here, too," Slocum said. "I'm afraid Young's men will go after her for helping me out. Someone must've seen her helping me out of town. That Sully sure knows what she did. Young'll be knowing before long if he don't know already."

"Oh, I'll be all right," Felicia said.

"No," said Jimson. "Slocum's right. You might not be safe in town. You'll stay here, too. You can help Molly out around here if it'll make you feel better about it. I'll send some boys into town after your things."

"Well, I—"

"It's settled," Jimson said.

Slocum tipped up his glass and emptied it. He handed it to Felicia, and he noticed tears in her eyes. He wondered if she had ever had a real home and how long it had been since people treated her simply like another human being.

"It's settled," he said.

3

Slocum was up and dressed the next day, but it had taken him an hour to get that way. He was still sore as hell. With the pain from the broken ribs, he knew that he couldn't fight anyone, not with fists or with guns. Any sudden movement of his arms shot terrible pains through his body. It was bad enough just finding a position in which he could sit and try to relax with a minimum amount of discomfort. Any movement, standing up, sitting down, turning, or looking over his shoulder, hurt. He would have to take it easy for a while. He didn't know just how long. And that meant he would have to lay low at Jimson's place and hope that the bastards over at Young's didn't find out about it.

That was a toss-up. They had beat him up and told him to leave town. They had left him on the floor of the stable. He was checked out of the hotel. He was gone from town, and his horse and saddle were gone from the stable. On the other hand, Felicia had disappeared from town, and someone might have seen her driving the wagon out toward Jimson's place with the big Appaloosa tied on the back. Sully, the weasly little stableman might even have told someone what had transpired. It seemed pretty obvious to Slocum

21

that the little shit had been told to get out for a while while Scarface and his playmates did their dirty deed, and he hadn't argued with them. He would likely run and tell them what had happened. Certainly if they asked him, he wouldn't hesitate to answer. It was therefore quite possible that they already knew the whole truth.

Slocum hoped that Young was not ready for an all-out war with Jimson and therefore would not come to the ranch, looking for him. He knew that he wouldn't be worth a shit in a real fight, not for a while yet. He sat on the porch of the ranch house, sipping coffee and smoking a cigar. Even the movement required for those simple tasks caused considerable pain. He watched the cowhands come and go, cursing his own enforced inactivity. The front door opened and Molly Jimson stepped out onto the porch, carrying a coffeepot. Slocum started to stand.

"Don't get up," she said. "Land sakes, here we are trying to get you all healed, and you go trying to act like a gentleman. Just sit there and take it easy. I just came out to check your cup. Looks like you could use a refill."

"Thank you, ma'am," Slocum said. "You're being too good to me."

"Nonsense," she said, pouring the coffee. "We'd do as much for anyone in trouble, especially if their trouble was with Parley Young. Besides, Carl told me why you're in trouble, so I feel like we're obligated."

"I appreciate it all the same," Slocum said. "How's Felicia doing?"

"Oh, she's doing fine," Molly said. "I always did like that girl, and I wished there had been some way to draw her away from that life she was leading. I'm grateful to you for doing that."

"It might not last," he said. "When the danger's over—"

"We'll just try everything we know how to make it last," Molly said. "She's really a very sweet young lady, and just now she's being very helpful to me. Well, I'd better get back inside and give her a hand. She'll be trying to do all my work for me."

Molly went back into the house. Slocum sat alone again. He puffed his cigar.

Jake Chrisman choused a half-dozen cows up out of a draw. He was a young cowhand, but he had worked for Carl Jimson already for several years. He liked his job, and he liked his boss. When he had first started with Jimson, he had been a green hand, but he had become a top-notch cowboy over the years, and he was proud of that fact. Riding in the dust of the cows, he topped the rise behind them. A rifle shot rang out, and Chrisman was knocked back out of his saddle. He hit the ground hard and did not move. More shots rang out, and soon the six head of cattle were lying scattered and dead on the prairie. A short distance away, Jerry Goodall, the scar-faced one, grinned and shoved his rifle into the scabbard on the side of his horse.

"Let's go, boys," he said. He turned his horse to leave the Jimson range, and Snider, Tallman, and Orwig followed.

It was later in the day when Charley Bouvier came riding slowly up to the ranch house, leading Chrisman's horse with the remains of Chrisman draped across the saddle. Slocum saw him coming and stood up with a groan. He could tell, even at a distance, what kind of burden Bouvier was leading. He walked into the house, where Jimson sat in his easy chair, smoking.

"Mr. Jimson," he said, "looks like bad news coming."

Jimson stood up and walked back out onto the porch with Slocum. Bouvier had hauled up just a few feet away. Jimson stopped and stared, his face suddenly ashen. "Jake?" he said.

"Yes sir," said Bouvier. "I found him out on the north range. There's six dead cows there, too. He must have just rounded them up, and someone surprised him."

"Shot?" Jimson said.

"Yes sir," Bouvier said. "Shot dead. Jake and the six cows. He never seen it coming. He didn't have his gun out or nothing."

"I've heard of rustlers shooting a man so they could run off the cattle," Slocum said, "but why would anyone shoot the cattle?"

"It's Parley Young," Jimson said. "The son of a bitch. He wants to run me off or run me out of business. If he stole the cattle, we could trace them to his place. So he killed them. There'll be more, but we'll be ready for him next time. Poor Jake. I never thought that Parley would go this far. Not cold-blooded, deliberate murder. Well, he won't get away with it. I swear he won't."

Molly came out onto the porch, followed by Felicia.

"Oh no," Molly said, seeing the body on the horse.

"It's started, Molly," said Jimson. "The war's started."

"Is that Jake Chrisman?" Felicia asked.

Bouvier nodded solemnly. "Yes, ma'am," he said. "It's Jake all right."

"Oh God," she said. She looked at Jimson with desperation on her face. "What are you going to do?"

"Take care of poor Jake first," Jimson said. "Charlie, ride into town and tell Merle what's happened out here. Take someone with you. I don't want anything to happen to you along the way. And before you go, tell someone to round up all the boys and get them over here to the house."

Jake Chrisman was laid out on a tabletop in the yard in front of the house, and the cowhands were all gathered around the porch when Bouvier came riding back with the sheriff from Harleyville. They stopped at the table, and Merle dismounted. Walking over to the body, he pulled back the blanket to take a look. He mounted up again and rode with Bouvier over to the porch. There both men dismounted. Merle stepped up on the porch and approached Jimson.

"I'm sorry about this, Carl," he said.

"You know who's responsible for it," Jimson said. "You know it as well as I do."

"I guess we've got a pretty good idea," Merle said, "but without witnesses or some kind of proof, you know there's nothing I can do. Oh, I'll ride out and have a talk with

Parley, but of course, he'll deny all knowledge of it."

"You know this means the start of a range war," said Jimson. "I can't just let this pass. You know that."

"Now, Carl," Merle said, "don't you go riding over to Parley's place to start anything."

"Hell, he's done started it," said Jimson, raising his voice. "You looked at poor Jake laying over there dead with a bullet in him. And there's six dead cows out there where Charley found him."

Merle looked over at Slocum where he sat. "I see you went and hired yourself that gunslinger," he said.

"What if I did?" Jimson snapped.

Slocum stood up with a groan and walked over to stand in front of the sheriff. "I'm not hired on here, Sheriff," he said. "I was fixing to leave town, and four men jumped me in the stable. They stove me up pretty bad. Broke some ribs. Mr. Jimson here was kind enough to take me in long enough to let me heal. That's all."

"Who were these men?" Merle asked.

"I'm a stranger here," said Slocum. "I don't know anyone, but they told me I'd better not go to work for Mr. Jimson."

"They was Young's men," said Jimson. "You know that as well as I do."

Merle looked again at Slocum. "Can you identify them?" he asked.

"I reckon I could," Slocum said. "One of these days I will."

"Now look here," Merle began, but Slocum cut him off.

"If I was to identify them for you," he said, "there'd be four of them calling me a liar, and you'd just say there's nothing you can do. So why bother?"

Merle turned to Jimson again. "I want to ride out and take a look at where it happened," he said.

"Charlie," said Jimson, "take him out there and show him—for all the good it'll do."

They watched in silence as Bouvier and Merle rode away from the ranch house. Then Jimson held up his hands for attention. All the cowhands stood silent.

"Boys," he said, "we're going to have us a funeral now. You all know what happened, and you know by now that we're fixing to get into a war with Parley Young and his bunch. Now, you all hired on to work cattle, not to fight a war, so any of you that wants to quit, there won't be no hard feelings. Come on up here on the porch, and I'll give you your pay."

No one moved. At last one young man stepped forward, hat in hand. "Mr. Jimson," he said, "we're all with you all the way."

"Charlie was our friend," said another. "We won't let him down or you."

"Could a been any one of us out there 'stead of Charlie," said another.

Jimson felt his eyes tear up. "Thank you, boys," he said. "Thank you."

Slocum was frustrated. Jimson had taken him in when he was hurt. Now Jimson was in trouble, and it was the kind of trouble that Slocum felt right at home with. Besides that, he had a personal debt to pay to Young and his gang, especially that scar-faced Jerry Goodall and his three cronies, but he was too stove up to be of any good to anyone. He cursed himself and his situation silently and ground his teeth in disgust. He thought a bit, and then he decided that he could do something. He walked over to Jimson's side.

"Mr. Jimson," he said, his voice low, "have you ever been in a war before?"

"No," said Jimson, "but, by God, I'll show that Parley Young that we can fight back. We ain't afraid of him."

"Can I make a suggestion?" Slocum asked.

"Go ahead," Jimson said.

"I've seen a few of these shooting wars," Slocum said. "Mostly from somewhere right in the middle, too. It seems to me that you'd be making a mistake by riding over to Young's place to strike back at him. In the first place, that's probably what he's hoping you'll do. Might even be why he had that poor boy out there killed—just to goad you into riding on over there after him. He'll be ready and waiting."

"So what do I do?" Jimson said. "Let him get away with it?"

"No," Slocum said, "but don't fall into his trap. How many ways are there he can ride in on you here?"

"Well"—Jimson scratched his head—"there's really only four approaches."

"Good," said Slocum. "Then if it was me, I'd post guards in those four places. He'll get anxious if you don't come riding into his trap right away, and he'll send someone over this way to pull another dirty trick. But you'll be ready for him this time and catch him in the act. Then that sheriff'll have to listen."

"Yeah," Jimson said. "Yeah. By God, Slocum, you're right. I should have thought of that myself, but I was too damn mad to think. Thanks, Slocum. I'll do it that way. I'll take care of it right away."

Jimson assigned watch positions to four men and sent them out to their posts right away. Then he set up a rotation so the four guards would be relieved on a regular schedule. With his plan put into effect, Slocum felt a little better about taking part in the defense of Jimson's range. If he couldn't fight just yet, at least he could be of some help. He'd sure had plenty of experience in that area. The men had been sent out with instructions to come riding fast back to the ranch house at the first sign of invasion by Young's men. They were located at strategic spots where they'd have a good long view of any approach. They would have time to carry the warning, and Jimson would have time to get a defense force ready for action. It was as good a plan as any, Slocum thought.

But he was itching for action. He made a motion as if to go for his Colt, but the pain stabbed him in the side. It was no use. For now, he would have to content himself with giving advice and hoping for the best. The gathering at last broke up, and Slocum found himself again alone on the porch. Jimson had followed some of the cowhands to the bunkhouse to give further instructions. There would be a burial soon. Felicia came out on the porch and took a chair beside Slocum.

"Do you mind?" she said.

"No," he said. "I'm glad for the company."

"Well," she said, "it looks like the trouble's started for real."

"It sure does look that way," Slocum said.

"Too bad you didn't make it on out of here like you planned," she said.

"Well, you know," he said, "I'm just as glad I didn't. I wish I wasn't so busted up though. I'd like to be of more help. When I rode into Harleyville, like I told you, I meant to rest up a bit and head on out. Then when I saw that there was trouble brewing around here, I did want to ride out away from it. Told myself I didn't need part of someone else's trouble. But now that it's starting and I'm here in the middle of it, I'm just as glad to be here."

She gave him a curious look. "How come?" she said.

"Well, let's just say that I don't like that Young's style," he said. "And I do like Mr. Jimson—and Molly. They're nice folks. I kind of like getting you out of that town, too. When I meet nice folks, I like for things to be good around them. Settled and peaceful."

He waited for her reaction to that last statement, but she sat silent. He glanced at her, but he couldn't read anything in the expression on her face.

"You want a glass of whiskey?" she asked him. "I know where it's at, and the Jimsons don't mind."

"I reckon it's late enough in the day," he said. "I sure wouldn't object."

"I'll be right back," she said, getting up to go into the house.

Slocum turned his head to watch her go, but the motion caused him pain. He straightened himself again and took a deep breath. He liked that girl. She could have been a fine lady under different circumstances. Maybe she would be after all. He wondered what had caused her to take up that life in the Red Ass Saloon. Oh, well, he thought, it's none of my business, but it was curious to think about how life dealt out different hands to different folks. He heard the door again, and Felicia came out with a glass and a bottle.

She poured some whiskey into the glass and handed it to Slocum.

"Thanks," he said, taking the glass. "You're not having any?"

"I didn't think it would look right," she said. "You know, me being a guest here in the Jimsons' house."

He held the glass out toward her. "You want a little taste?" he asked her. She grinned and took the glass, tipping it up for a swallow. Then she handed it back to Slocum. He took a healthy gulp. "Thanks," she said. "Slocum?"

"Yeah?"

"How's this all going to work out? This fight and all. Parley Young's got a bunch of bad men over at his place. Gunfighters and thugs. All Carl's got are just cowboys."

"If they do what we told them to do," Slocum said, "they ought to be all right, and if they can just hold off Young's gang till I can get around better again, why, I'll pitch in and do my share."

"Are you a professional gunfighter, Slocum?" she asked.

"I have been," he said. "I've done a lot of things in my time. I don't normally hire out to do killing, but I can sure hold my own in a fight."

"You a cowhand?" she said.

"I've done that, too," he told her.

He turned down the rest of his drink, and Felicia poured him another. Just then Molly Jimson came out to join them. She pulled up a chair and sat down.

"Well, how are you feeling?" she asked Slocum.

"Just fine till I try to move," he said. "I sure do hate being a burden on you like this."

"Now just hush that kind of talk," Molly said. "You're no burden. I heard you when you told Carl not to go riding over to the Young place. I'm glad you were here. He wouldn't have listened to anyone else. Not me. Not Merle, and not any of the hands. I'm glad you're here. It's a comfort."

"Well, thank you, ma'am," Slocum said. "I'm glad you feel that way, and I'll try to help out any way I can."

The burial took place about an hour later, and when it

was over and done, a somber crowd scattered in various directions. The Jimsons, Felicia, and Slocum went back to the house. Most of the cowhands went to the bunkhouse. Some went in other directions. Molly went on inside the house, and Felicia followed her. Slocum and Jimson sat on the porch. They lit cigars and smoked in silence. Molly brought out the whiskey and two glasses, then went back inside. The two men drank and smoked for a while in silence. At last, Jimson spoke.

"Slocum," he said, "when do you reckon they'll hit us again?"

"There's no telling, Mr. Jimson," Slocum said. "I figure they'll wait awhile for you to come riding over there, like I said. But just how long they'll wait, I can't say. It's almost for sure though, that they'll come riding back here when their patience runs thin. They could come in full force, or they could send another small harrassing group like they did the last time—still try to goad you into coming at them—riding into their trap."

"Well, either way," Jimson said, "we'll be ready for the sons of bitches. Thanks to you."

"Can your boys handle their shooters?" Slocum asked.

"They can handle them as good as most cowhands," Jimson said, "but they ain't gunfighters, if that's what you mean."

"They don't need to be gunfighters," Slocum said. "They need to be able to lay an ambush and take a good aim with a rifle. They won't be facing anyone down for a shoot-out."

"They can handle it," Jimson said. "They're good boys."

"What we need to do is keep the surprise on our side from now on," Slocum said. "Young surprised us the first time. We can't let that happen again."

Jimson looked at Slocum and smiled. "I notice you said we," he said. "I like that."

Slocum mused to himself. *I did, didn't I,* he thought. *I guess, by God, I have made this my fight after all.*

4

It was four days later when Buttermilk Smith was standing watch behind a large boulder along the way into the Jimson Ranch from the northwest. Smith was not much more than a kid, but he had worked for Carl Jimson already for three years. He had come to Jimson broke and out of work, just a kid who needed a job real bad, and Jimson had taken him on. Now he'd had a steady job for three years, was even saving money, and he was very proud of that fact. He was also, like the rest of Jimson's boys, fiercely loyal to Jimson. He wore a six-gun strapped around his waist, and he carried a rifle in a saddle boot, and he was ready and willing to use either one to defend the rights of his employer.

Enough time had gone by quietly since the alarm with nothing out of the ordinary happening that the boys were beginning to relax again, and Smith had just rolled and lit a cigarette. He took one long and relaxed draw. Then he saw the distant dust cloud. He sat up alert and watched. It was moving in his direction. Soon after that, he could tell that six riders were coming fast. He ran to his horse and practically jumped onto its back, kicking it in the sides and heading for the ranch house as fast as he could make the horse go. In a short time he came tearing into the yard in front of the house. Slocum was sitting there on the porch. He stood up at the sight of Smith barreling in.

"Where's Mr. Jimson?" the boy shouted.

Having heard the commotion, Jimson came out onto the porch without being called. "Right here, Buttermilk," he said. "What the hell's up?"

"Six riders coming hard from the northwest," Smith shouted.

"Get yourself a fresh horse," Jimson told the cowboy. "I'll get some more of the boys."

"I'll ride along with you on this one, if you don't mind," said Slocum, getting up out of his chair. He felt like he had undergone a long-enough period of enforced idleness, and he at least needed to move around some. He was still stiff and sore, but he was hoping that a little action might help work it out and loosen him up.

"Come on ahead," Jimson said, "if you think you're up to it."

Out at the corral, horses were saddled hurriedly. Slocum tried to swing the saddle up onto his big Appaloosa, but he was unable to do it, and a cowhand tossed it up on the horse's back for him. Irritated at himself, he cinched it up and mounted, wincing with a little pain, and soon a dozen men, including Jimson and Slocum, were mounted and riding. Jimson had a spot in mind where he wanted to meet up with the intruders, a place where the trail narrowed and high walls were on both sides. He figured he had time to make it there before the riders from Young's outfit did. They rode hard. Slocum felt the jarring in his rib cage with every movement of his big Appaloosa. He wasn't at all sure that he would be able to do anyone any good on this trip, but he couldn't stand much more of the sitting around, and it would be a start. He clenched his teeth and bore the pain.

When they reached the spot for the planned ambush, Jimson issued hurried orders. "Get your horses back out of sight," he said, "and then hunker your ass down here along the edge. When you see them coming, wait for my shot. We'll shoot the ground in front of them and try to make them stop. Try to scare them back home. I don't want any killing here if we can keep from it."

All the boys did as they were told, and soon they were waiting for the Young riders, rifles ready, trigger fingers itching for action. Slocum was lying on the ground beside Jimson with his Winchester in his hands. He had a shell cranked into the chamber, but he wasn't at all sure he would be able to fire it with any accuracy. He was just as glad that his first shot was not supposed to count. Soon the riders came into view. Jimson waited until they were almost below him. Then he fired a shot into the ground in front of them, and a dozen more shots rang out. The gang beneath them reined in their horses, and the frightened mounts nickered and stamped around in confusion. Slocum's ribs ached with the impact of the rifle against his shoulder.

The riders down below fought to regain control of their nervous horses or gave up and dismounted to run for cover, pulling six-guns and rifles as they scurried for nonexistent holes to crawl into. Some still tried to control horses, while others looked around for something up above themselves to shoot back at. Jimson called out to his hands to stop firing, and then he shouted to the invaders in a loud voice.

"Turn around and go right back where you come from," he said, "and there won't be no killing here today. And when you get back, tell your boss that if you try it again, I won't shout no warning. Tell him next time we'll shoot to kill first. Tell him that we're ready for you over here."

One of the Young gang panicked, raised a rifle to his shoulder, and fired a wild shot up at the ledge. Jimson fired back immediately and dropped the man dead with one shot. The others down there on the trail all raised their hands. One called out, "Don't shoot. Don't shoot. We're going."

"Take that dumb one along with you," Jimson said. "He won't get buried here."

Two of the invaders loaded the body on the horse it had left behind, and soon all the gang was on its way back toward Harleyville and eventually the Young spread. They had accomplished nothing. Young's plan of continued harrassment had met with a prepared force and had been driven off. Jimson and the others stood and watched them go. The young cowhands sent up a cheer. Jimson let them have their fun, and then when they were quiet again, he said, "That cheering is somewhat premature, boys. They'll be back, but next time they'll know that we're waiting. They'll try something different."

"You could have thinned his ranks by six instead of just one," Slocum said to Jimson in a low voice. "There'd be six less to deal with next time."

"I could have," said Jimson, "but I don't operate that way. War's been declared now, they've got fair warning, and next time we'll shoot first and talk later. Let's go."

He sent another guard back to the spot from which Buttermilk Smith had been watching, even though he thought it unlikely that anyone would ride up that way again anytime soon. Then the rest of them rode back to the ranch house. His Appaloosa taken care of, Slocum took up his spot on the porch again. He was sore from the ride, but he was glad he had gone along. He figured that he needed to be doing something to loosen himself up again, needed to be as active as he could manage in order to get himself back in shape as soon as possible. He had just settled himself down when Felicia came out of the house.

"What happened?" she asked him.

"We ran them off," Slocum said. "Jimson killed one of them that shot at him first."

"Do you think they'll try again?" she asked.

"I'd bet money on it," he said.

"You think there's going to be a range war?"

"Mr. Jimson said that war was declared out there today," Slocum told her. "I guess that means we're in it now already."

"Are you staying?"

"I won't run out now."

"How do you feel?" she said. "I mean, after taking a ride like that and all."

"It gave me some pain," Slocum said, "but I made it all right."

He saw Jimson coming from the corral with one of the

cowhands. They were both on fresh mounts. Riding slow past the porch, the ranch boss said, "In case anyone should ask, I'm going into town to see Merle and report what happened out here."

"Do you think that's a safe thing to do?" Slocum asked.

"I don't think Young will try anything more today, especially not right out in the open," Jimson said. "Tell Molly not to worry. We'll be back here before dark."

Molly stepped out onto the porch just as the two riders were disappearing in a dust cloud. "Is that Carl?" she said.

"Yes, ma'am," said Slocum.

"Where's he going?" she asked.

"Said he was going in to see the sheriff to report what happened out here," Slocum said.

"What did happen?" Molly asked. "Nobody's told me anything."

Slocum told the tale once again.

"Oh, dear," she said. "I hope nothing happens to him."

"He should be all right, ma'am," said Slocum. "Like he said, Young's not likely to pull anything out in the open."

"I hope he's right about that," Molly said. "Oh well, you want a cup of coffee?"

"That would be nice," said Slocum.

As Molly headed back into the house, Felicia jumped up to follow her. "I'll fetch it out," she said.

In Harleyville, when Jimson and his hand pulled up in front of the sheriff's office, they saw the Young horses already tied to the hitching rail out front. They gave each other a hard look, tied their own mounts, and went inside the office. Young was there with two of the men who had attempted the invasion. The men from the Young Ranch and the two from Jimson's stood silent and stared hard at each other. After an awkward and tense moment of silence, the sheriff spoke up.

"Parley here says you killed one of his men today, Carl," Merle said.

"I damn sure did," said Jimson. "He fired the first shot. He was on my range with five other hands from Young's outfit. I told them to get off my property, and there wouldn't be no killing. That one didn't listen so good, so I brought him down. That's what we come in here to tell you about."

"They was just chasing strays," said Young. "That's all."

"They was moving awful fast," said Jimson. "I never seen anyone hunt strays like that. That when I told them to ride back out, that one took a shot at me."

"Well," Merle said, "we got no proof they weren't just hunting strays, Carl, and the one that did break the law and shot at you, if you're telling the truth about that, is dead. I guess there's nothing more to be done about it. But I want you two to back off each other. You hear me? I don't want a range war to deal with here. Now, there's been a killing on each side. Don't you think that's enough? I want it stopped. I want it stopped now before it goes any further, and I mean that."

"I don't know anything about who killed that boy out on Carl's range," said Young, "but I do know who killed Grote Foss just today."   •

"He was on my land," said Jimson, "and he shot at me first. I've got plenty of witnesses."

"I'll bet you have," said Young.

"That's enough of that," Merle snapped. "I done told you. I won't have it. Both of you cut it out. Call it even before things get out of hand. All of you go on back home now. Go on. Get out of here."

Jimson turned to the cowboy standing beside him. "Come on," he said. "We're wasting our time in here."

Back at the ranch with the sun low in the western sky, Jimson broke out the whiskey bottle and joined Slocum on the porch. He poured two drinks and handed one to Slocum.

"Wasted trip," he said.

"The sheriff won't do anything?" Slocum asked.

"He took their word that they was just chasing strays," said Jimson. "Chasing strays. Bullshit."

"I never did have much use for the law," Slocum said. "I just try to stay out of its way is all."

"I should have played it your way out there today," said Jimson. "Should have killed them all. The bodies would have been on my land, and there wouldn't be no one left alive to claim they'd been chasing strays. Goddamn Merle."

"There'll be another chance," said Slocum. "There's no doubt about that."

"But after what happened today," Jimson said, "you don't think they'll come riding in here like that again, do you?"

"Not like that," said Slocum. "They'll find another way. They'll come in quiet. Maybe at night. They'll try to slip up on a rider out alone, the way they did the first time. Killing one at a time won't get things done very fast, but it will keep you on edge. Might smoke you out."

"Maybe I ought to be smoked out," Jimson said. "Maybe I ought to get a dozen boys and ride right on over there to his place and take him on out in the open and have it out and get it over with and done."

"I don't think so," Slocum said. "I'd say, wait a few more days and see what he tries next. I'd say, if there's any killing, let it happen over here so we can prove that it was him that came looking for trouble."

"Oh, hell," said Jimson, "you're probably right again. I should have listened to you before. I will listen now. So what do I do?"

"Just what you've been doing," Slocum said. "Keep those guards out, and tell those boys when they're standing watch to keep real alert. Tell them we don't know what he might try to pull next. Tell them to be ready for anything, and to expect a sneak attack next time."

"I'll tell them," Jimson said. He drained his glass and poured another drink for himself. Looking over at Slocum's glass, he saw that it needed refilling, too, so he poured another for Slocum.

"Thanks," Slocum said. "This is good whiskey."

"The best," said Jimson. "Slocum, when I first met you, I said something about not needing to hire gunfighters."

"I remember," said Slocum.

"Well, I'm sorry if what I said offended you in any way."

"Don't worry about it," Slocum said.

"I just want to say right now, that I'm damn glad you're here."

"You know," Slocum said, "considering all the circumstances, I am, too."

He sipped some more of the good whiskey and enjoyed the sensation of it burning its way down his throat. *Marvelous,* he thought, *how something can burn and be smooth at the same time.* But there were other things on his mind, things more important, if not more immediate. Here he was in the middle of a war, and he wasn't even familiar with the terrain.

"Mr. Jimson," he said, "can I borrow one of your hands tomorrow?"

"Well, sure," said Jimson, "I reckon, but what for?"

"I want to ride out and get the feel of your range," Slocum said. "Try to get familiar with the surroundings."

"Well," Jimson said, "you went out and took a pretty good ride today. I guess you know if you're up to it or not."

"I won't say that ride today didn't jar me some," Slocum said, "but I made it all right. I guess I can stand some more of it."

"You can take ole Buttermilk along with you," Jimson said. "He knows the spread real good, and he's easy to get on with. I'll tell him to go along with you tomorrow."

"Thanks," Slocum said. "He's the young fellow that came riding in with the warning today. Right?"

"That's right. Buttermilk Smith. He's a good hand. Reliable and loyal. Well, all of them are. They're all good boys."

"Buttermilk will do just fine," Slocum said. He thought about the way these hands seemed to look up to old Jimson almost like a father, and then he thought that it made sense. Jimson seemed to act like they were all his sons. Slocum had the sense that Jimson had gathered up a bunch of strays and given them homes, and because of that, they would do anything for him. He kept all those thoughts to himself though, and he and Jimson sipped their whiskey a few moments in silence, before Jimson spoke up again.

"Slocum," he said, "you know, this ain't your fight, and if you was to take a mind to ride off from it, I wouldn't hold it against you none."

"I know you wouldn't, Mr. Jimson," said Slocum. "But with all that's happened around here, I've decided to make it my fight. Besides, I like your whiskey."

"Then hold your glass over here, by God," Jimson said. "Hell, pard, we might just as well get our ass good and drunk tonight. What do you say?"

"It might be our last chance for a spell," Slocum said. "Sounds like a good idea to me."

In the Red Ass Saloon, Jerry Goodman sat at a table with his boss. Young refilled their two glasses and leaned forward conspiratorially, speaking in a low voice. "They won't be looking for us again so soon," he said. "I want you to hit them tonight."

"Where at?" Goodman asked.

"The same place," said Young. "That's the last thing they'll be looking for. Now you know where they have that guard posted. Don't ride in hard and fast this time. Go sneaking in well after dark. Sneak around behind that guard and kill him. Then ride on in if it looks like the coast is clear and kill a few more cows. Or run them off if the coast is clear enough."

"You don't want us to ride on in to the ranch house?" Goodman said.

"It's most likely going to be well guarded," Young said. "Don't take no chances. My plan for right now is to just pester ole Jimson to death. When he's had enough of it, he'll cave in. He'll sell out cheap or just get the hell out, running for his life."

"He didn't seem about to run today," Goodman said.

"I didn't figure on him laying that trap the way he done," said Young. "That was my mistake, but I don't aim to make another one. I was getting too anxious, I guess. So we'll just do what we done before. Keep on picking at him. First one place, then another. If he keeps trying to hold out, he'll wake up one morning and find out that all his cowhands are either dead or run out on him."

"I'm wondering about that Slocum," said Goodman. "His horse is gone, but so is that whore Felicia."

"So she rode out with him," said Young. "They took a liking to each other right off. We seen that. Hell, he killed ole Toughnut over her, and that was all it took for her to fall over dead in love with him. They're both long gone. Don't give them another thought."

5

Jerry Goodall, Buck Snider, Jody Tallman, and Red Orwig rode quietly and slowly onto the Jimson spread. It was well after dark, but the trail was clear and easy to follow. They knew where the danger spots would be, and they thought that they'd have a fairly easy time of it, because of the fact that they were retracing the same steps they had made earlier that day. Anyhow, that was Parley Young's intention and his plan. Snider rolled himself a smoke, stuck it between his lips, and struck a match on the thigh of his jeans. He was holding the match to the end of his cigarette when Goodall spoke in a harsh whisper.

"Put that son of a bitch out," he said. "We're trying to sneak in here, you know."

Snider threw the cigarette down and scowled.

"Jerry," said Tallman, "how much farther you reckon?"

"Not much," Goodall said. "In fact, I don't want no more talking from here out. I think we'll swing off the trail just a little ways up there and see if we can ride up behind that guard they posted. Keep as quiet as you can, and don't light no fucking cigarettes."

Just as Goodall had said, soon he led the other three off the trail. He took a wide swing to make sure that they did not alert the man on watch. Eventually, he called a halt, and he dismounted. "Wait here," he whispered, and he started walking back toward the trail. It was a longer walk than Goodall was used to making, and before he came to the end of it, his feet were hurting. But he found the guard just where he had expected to find him.

Young Joeboy Grayson sat cross-legged on top of a boulder overlooking the trail below. Goodall moved closer, slipping a knife out of a scabbard at his waist. He took another step, and he was afraid the noise of his footfall could be heard for miles. He stood still for a moment. Grayson did not move. He had not heard. Goodall took another careful step and hesitated again. Still Grayson did not indicate that he had heard anything, but Goodall was getting closer now, and his steps would have to be even more careful. He decided to make a bold move. He was fairly confident in his ability, so he took the knife by its blade, raised it over his shoulder, and threw it with a hard and powerful swing. It thudded into Grayson's back between his shoulder blades.

Grayson cried out in surprise and pain, but the blade did not kill him right away. He turned and fired his rifle, the shot creasing the right side of Goodall's cheek and tearing his right ear in half. Goodall shrieked and grabbed for his ear. He felt hot blood gush from the torn ear and run down his neck and his arm. His defensive instincts overcame his first reaction, and he reached for his six-gun with a sticky right hand, but before he could pull it, Joeboy Grayson pitched forward and lay dead on his face. Goodall cursed vilely. He pulled the bandanna from around his neck and held it against the side of his head. Then he stepped over to the body to retrieve his deadly knife.

Yanking it loose, he wiped the blade clean on the dead man's jeans, then put it away. He daubed at the side of his head with the bandanna and cursed some more. "Son of a bitch," he said, and he shoved the body with the toe of his boot until it rolled over the edge of the boulder and fell down onto the trail below. Then he started walking back to where he had left his horse with the other riders. Reaching them at last, he mounted up, grumbling to himself. Snider said, "What's wrong, Jerry?"

"Shut up," Goodall said. "Let's go kill some cows."

Bennie Wellman rode out to the boulder where he was scheduled to relieve Joeboy Grayson. He had left the trail some distance before arriving at the boulder, and he rode up to it as the eastern sky was beginning to light up for the morning. He did not see Joeboy, and he sensed that something was wrong. Joeboy's horse grazed contentedly not far away. Bennie left his own horse there with it and dismounted. Drawing the rifle out of his scabbard, he approached the boulder cautiously. There was still no sign of Joeboy, but when he had gotten close enough to the boulder, he could see the blood.

He looked around himself carefully in all directions, but he could see no sign of anyone anywhere around. He moved onto the boulder and looked more closely. He was certain that he was looking at bloodstains there, quite a lot of blood, too. He moved closer to the edge and looked down, and then he saw the body there. He hurried back to his horse, mounted up, and leading Joeboy's abandoned horse, rode around and down onto the trail. He discovered the worst. It was Joeboy, all right. Loading the body onto the horse, he headed back for the ranch house.

Slocum had already mounted up and ridden out with Buttermilk Smith by the time Bennie Wellman rode in. It was Felicia who saw him coming, and she went back into the house to fetch out Mr. Jimson. Jimson studied the corpse for a moment in silence. Then he told Wellman, "Get Charlie Bouvier and a couple other boys. We're riding into town." Molly stepped out onto the porch wringing her hands as Wellman rode away toward the corral. She took in the situation in a couple of seconds.

"Carl," she said, "where are you going?"

"I ought to be riding over to Young's place with all hands," he said, "but I ain't. I mean to give Merle one last chance to do things according to the law."

"Don't go, Carl," she said. "Wait for Slocum."

"He's liable to be gone all day," said Jimson. "This can't wait. Besides, if you're thinking there might be trouble, hell, ole Slocum ain't yet fit for a fight."

"Don't start anything, Carl," she said.

"It's already been started," he snapped back at her. Then he took a deep breath and said more calmly, "I ain't going to start nothing, Molly. I'm just going in to see Merle and tell him what happened here. That's all."

Wellman came back leading a saddled horse for Jimson, and Bouvier and two more hands rode behind him. Jimson climbed onto the extra horse, and the five men rode off in the direction of town.

Slocum and Buttermilk Smith rode toward the boulder where Joeboy had been killed. "Right up there is where one of our boys is standing watch," Buttermilk said.

"Let's go on over and see if he's got anything to report," said Slocum. They rode onto the rock and found it abandoned. They also found the bloodstains.

"This don't look good," Buttermilk said. "Joeboy should have been relieved by this time."

"Likely whoever came out to relieve him found the body," said Slocum. "Probably loaded him up and took him back in. Let's get back to the ranch house and find out what's going on."

Jimson and his riders found Merle in the Red Ass Saloon, having a cold beer. He was standing alone at the bar, so Jimson stepped up to stand to his right. Bouvier and the other cowhands stood at the bar to the sheriff's left. Merle looked from Jimson to the cowhands a bit nervously. "What's this all about?" he said.

"If you'll step out in the street you'll see," said Jimson.

"What'll I see?" Merle asked.

"Poor Joeboy Grayson," said Jimson, "slung across his saddle. Someone stuck him in the back with a knife."

Merle tipped up his glass and drained it of beer. Then he smacked it down on the bar and headed for the door.

Jimson and the cowboys followed him. Outside, Merle looked grimly at the body. "Anyone see what happened?" he asked.

" 'Course not," said Jimson. "Joeboy was standing watch out on the trail. When Bennie here went out to relieve him, this is what he found."

"Well, I'll ride out to Parley's place and have a talk with him," Merle said.

"He'll just deny any knowledge of it," said Jimson. "What the hell good will that do?"

"I'm sure you're right about that, Carl," said Merle, "but I can check around and try to find out where all his men were at during the night. After I've had a talk with him, I'll come out to your place. Might be we can find some kind of evidence around where it happened. Tell your boys to steer clear of the place. There might could be some kind of distinctive tracks or something. We don't want them to get messed up."

"Damn it, Merle," Jimson started, but Merle interrupted him.

"I know what you're thinking, Carl," he said, "but we got to have proof. If you weren't so upset, you'd understand that. Now I'm riding out to Young's ranch, and I'll be out to see you after that. Go on back home now and wait for me."

Jimson was raging inside, but he did as he was told. He and the boys were headed back toward the ranch when they saw Slocum and Buttermilk Smith riding toward them. They reined up and waited till the two came up to them. Buttermilk recognized the body on the horse right away.

"We was afraid of that," he said. "We seen the blood."

"How'd it happen?" Slocum asked.

"Knife in the back," said Jimson. "Bennie found him and brought him in."

"There's more dead cattle out there, too," Slocum said. "We came across them on our way back to the ranch house."

"What're you doing here?" Jimson asked.

"Mrs. Jimson told us you headed into town," Slocum

said. "We thought we'd better try to join up with you—just in case."

"Well, I'm obliged," said Jimson, "but you wasted a trip. Merle told us to go back home. Says he's going to have a talk with Parley Young, then come out to my place and look around for some kind of evidence. I think he's wasting his time, too."

"Likely you're right about that," Slocum agreed. "What do you want to do next?"

"Hell, Slocum, I don't know. This whole mess is making me feel mighty old and useless."

"Let's ride on back to your place and make some plans," Slocum said.

Parley Young, Jerry Goodall, and the others stood on the porch of the rambling Young ranch house, watching the sheriff ride toward them. Goodall and the others tested the slide of their revolvers in the holsters. Goodall sneered.

"Anyone see you last night?" Young asked.

"No one," said Goodall.

"Then just keep quiet and let me handle ole Merle," Young said.

Merle rode up and dismounted. He stepped toward the porch. "Howdy, Parley," he said.

"Good afternoon, Merle," said Young. "What brings you all the way out here?"

"There was another killing out at Jimson's place last night," the sheriff said. "Joeboy Grayson. Someone put a knife in his back."

He glanced at the knife strapped to the belt around Goodall's waist, and Goodall, taking notice, snarled.

"That's too bad," said Young. "I never got to know the boy very well, but he seemed like a nice young man. You got any ideas who might have done it?"

"Carl Jimson thinks you might have an idea," Merle said.

"He would think that," said Young. "I'm getting tired of Carl accusing me of every damn thing that goes wrong out at his place. Hell, Merle, his boys could be fighting among themselves. Or there could be a third party trying to stir up trouble between me and ole Carl. He's got no reason to go accusing me. No reason at all."

"You know where all your hands was at all night last night?" Merle asked.

"They was all right here all night," Young said.

"How can you be sure of that?" Merle asked.

"We had us an all-night poker game going," said Young. "They was all here all night."

Merle walked in closer and looked straight at Goodall. "What happened to the side of your head?" he asked.

"Steer horn caught it," Goodall said.

Merle stepped up on the porch for a better look.

"Looks more like a bullet grazed it to me," he said. "Cut your damned ear in half, too, didn't it?"

"It was a steer horn," said Goodall. "I told you."

Snider took a step forward then, and said, "I seen it happen. Steer horn. That's what it was."

"Yeah," said Merle. He turned to face Young again. "I hope you're not lying to me, Parley," he said, " 'cause if you are, I'll find out sooner or later, and when I do, I'll be coming after your ass."

"You got no call to talk to me like that, Merle," said Young as the sheriff turned his back on him to walk over to his waiting horse. "You get yourself some kind of proof of wrongdoing before you come talking to me like that. I don't want to listen to no more groundless accusations. Not from Carl Jimson and not from you. You hear me?"

Merle ignored Young's outcry and reached for his saddle horn. Just then Jerry Goodall pulled the Colt from his holster, thumbed back the hammer, leveled the six-gun at Merle's back, and pulled the trigger. The sheriff flinched, stiffened, drew his own revolver, and turned, but a second shot from Goodall smashed into his chest. His frightened horse turned and ran as his lifeless body crumpled to the ground.

Young whirled on Goodall, startled and unbelieving. "You dumb bastard," he shouted. "What the hell did you do that for?"

"The son of a bitch was on to us," Goodall said.

"There wasn't a damn thing he could do," said Young. "Wasn't you listening to what I said? He didn't have no evidence."

"I heard what you said, all right," said Goodall, "but I heard what he was saying, too. Maybe I heard better than you did. He was on to us, all right, and he was after us. I thought it best to stop him before he come any closer. That's all."

"You ain't paid to think," Young said. "I do the thinking around here. You hear me? You just do what I tell you to do and nothing else and leave the thinking all to me. Goddamn it, you dumb dumb bastard, now—"

Young shut up suddenly as Goodall pulled his Colt again and aimed it at Young's chest. Young stood still, his face turned white, his eyes wide, and his mouth hanging open.

"Shut up," Goodall said. "I don't let nobody call me names like that. You don't pay me enough so you can call me names. I done what I thought was best. That's all, so don't go calling me names over it, or the next time I'll kill you just as dead as I killed that damn sheriff."

"All right, Jerry," Young said. "All right. Don't get excited now. I was just a little upset is all. I didn't mean nothing by it. We just got to figure out what to do next is all. We got to figure out what to do with him. Now put your gun down. Maybe we can make this work out to our good after all. Okay?"

Goodall eased the hammer down on his Colt and dropped the six-gun back into its holster. He still stared at Young with a hard look. "That's easy enough to figure out," he said. "What to do with him. We'll just take him over to Jimson's place and dump him there. How'll it look when the dead sheriff is found on Jimson's place? Huh? How'll that look?"

"All right," Young said. "Have someone catch up to his horse, and then load him up on it. Put them in the barn till dark. Then you can send someone off to Jimson's with him—just like you said. That's a good idea, Jerry. Good idea."

"See?" said Goodall. "I ain't so bad at thinking after all, am I?"

As Goodall turned away to take care of the problem, Parley Young breathed a sigh of relief and wiped his forehead with his sleeve. He realized that he would have to be very careful in the way he handled Goodall from this point on. Goodall was like a cannon with a short fuse. He was crazy, and he was dangerous.

Slocum pulled his Colt. He eased the hammer back down, reholstered, and pulled again. He was slow. It still hurt his ribs some to make that kind of motion. And the faster the motion, the more it pained him. He did it again and again, though. He needed to overcome the pain—or work it out. He knew that something was going to happen that would require his participation, and he knew that it was going to happen soon. The war was on. The showdown was coming.

He agreed with Carl Jimson that the law was not going to do anything about the killings that had taken place—the killing of men and the killing of cattle. He also agreed with Jimson that there could be no one behind it all other than Parley Young. He himself had experienced the tactics of Young when Goodall and the others had jumped him in the stable in Harleyville. Slocum figured that he would be going into action one way or the other very soon. He hoped that the Young gang did not know he was still around. If that was the case, then he would have an edge on them. His very appearance would be a surprise. That would help. But would it be enough to overcome his loss of speed with his Colt? He couldn't count on that. He would have to find other ways to make up for that loss.

He tried his draw a few more times, then headed back for the porch of the Jimson ranch house. He found Carl Jimson sitting with a glass and bottle. Another glass sat on the porch rail. Slocum walked up on the porch and took a seat.

"Where you been?" Jimson asked him.

"Oh, just trying to limber up my gun arm," Slocum said.

"Glass is waiting for you," said Jimson, motioning toward the empty one on the rail. Slocum reached for it and picked it up. Jimson held the bottle out toward it and poured a glass full for Slocum. "Thanks," Slocum said. He tipped the glass up and took a sip.

"It's going to be dark soon," said Jimson.

"Yeah," Slocum agreed.

"Merle should've been here by now," Jimson said. "He ain't coming. He wouldn't ride out this late. It would throw him well after dark when he headed back. Besides, he said he wanted to look over the scene of the killing. Wouldn't do no good to look it over after dark. He ain't coming."

"Maybe he'll get around in the morning," Slocum said.

"Maybe not," said Jimson. "You know what I'm thinking? I'm thinking about where he went before he meant to come out here. I'm thinking he rode out to Parley Young's place to question him about the killings out here. I'm thinking that ole Merle might not be coming around here at all—ever."

"You think Young is dumb enough to kill a lawman?" Slocum said. "I don't think so. He might have talked longer than he expected to over there. Hell, anything might have throwed him later than what he thought. He'll likely ride out here in the morning."

"I got a bad feeling," said Jimson. "I don't think he's coming."

Slocum shrugged. "Well," he said, "we'll see."

"So how is it?" Jimson asked.

"How's what?" said Slocum.

"The gun arm," Jimson said. "How's it coming along?"

"Oh," Slocum said. "It's coming."

6

Jerry Goodall, Buck Snider, Jody Tallman, and Red Orwig
rode back onto the Jimson ranch. They rode under cover
of darkness, and they led the late sheriff's horse along behind them. The sheriff's body was slung across the saddle.
Parley Young had told Goodall to get rid of the body, but
the rest of the plan was Goodall's. He had not even told
his three riding companions. He meant to dump the sheriff's body on Jimson's ranch, and turn the sheriff's horse
loose over there. Then he meant to ride clear into the ranch
house and start shooting. It wouldn't matter too much, he
thought, if no one even got hit. But when Jimson and his
men started shooting back, Goodall and his bunch would
skeedaddle. When anyone looked around at daylight, they
would discover the dead sheriff. Goodall was proud of himself. It was a good plan, he thought. With the sheriff's horse
and body found on the Jimson ranch, the finger of guilt
would point to Jimson.

Goodall was not riding in by the same route he had used
on the two previous invasions. He was riding a more south-
erly route. He figured they'd be watching that way more
carefully than ever. The south ground was flatter and clearer,
and a horse and rider could be seen from quite a distance

away, at least in the daytime. But unknown to Goodall, Charley Bouvier was crouched behind a clump of wahoo brush, and he saw the riders coming. He started to jump on his horse and race for the ranch house. Those were his instructions. But the riders were coming fast, and he decided to try to slow them down some before taking off. He raised his rifle to his shoulder and took careful aim. Then he squeezed the trigger.

Buck Snider screamed as he felt the hot lead rip through his shoulder. He grabbed for the wound and felt the hot, sticky blood ooze between his fingers. "I'm shot," he cried. "Oh damn. I'm hurt." All four riders reined in their horses. The other three jerked out their guns. They looked around them in the darkness but saw no one. "Where is he?" Tallman said in a desperate voice. Orwig said, "I don't see no one."

"Well, the son of a bitch sure seen us," snapped Goodall. "Find him, goddamn it. Find him."

They heard the pounding hooves first. Then they looked and saw the distant rider racing away from them. They saw him only for an instant as he rode into the darkness. "There he is," Tallman said. "Let's go."

"Hold on," said Goodall, "you dumb shit. We'll never catch him in this dark, and besides, he'll be going for help. We don't know how far back they might be waiting. We've lost our surprise now anyhow. Dump ole Merle's ass out of his saddle and let's make tracks. We'll hit their ranch house another time."

Tallman rode back beside the sheriff's horse and took hold of the body by the waistband of the trousers. Then he dragged it until it slipped off the horse. It landed hard with a dull and sickening thud. A small cloud of dust rose up around it.

"Let's get the hell out of here," Goodall said.

"I'm bleeding real bad here, Jerry," Snider whined. "Ain't you going to do nothing to help me?"

"Shut up and ride," said Goodall. "Ain't nothing we can do for you out here."

Tallman glanced back down at the body he had just dumped. "So long, Merle," he said.

Buttermilk Smith was the first one at the bunkhouse to hear Bouvier riding in. He was dressed and ready to go out to relieve one of the guards, so he ran out to see what was happening. Bouvier told him, and the two of them hurried on over to the ranch house. Slocum heard the racket and pulled on his trousers. As he was walking toward the front door, Jimson came from his room.

"What is it?" Jimson asked.

"Don't know," said Slocum. "Let's find out."

He opened the door and the two of them went out onto the porch.

"Riders was coming in on the south trail," Bouvier said when he saw his boss on the porch. "I took a shot at them to slow them down. Then I hurried on back here."

"Get our horses, Buttermilk," said Jimson. Then he turned to Slocum. "Come on. Let's get dressed," he said.

In a few minutes Carl Jimson, Slocum, Buttermilk Smith, and Charley Bouvier were riding toward the south trail.

"How many riders you see?" Jimson asked Bouvier.

"Well, sir," Bouvier said, "it's dark, so I could be wrong, but I think I seen four riders and one horse without no rider."

"What the hell would they be doing with one extra horse?" Buttermilk said.

No one answered. They rode on in silence until they arrived at the spot where Bouvier had been watching. He pointed off to the west. "They was coming from there," he said.

"We didn't meet them anywhere," Jimson said. "You must have drove them off with your shot. Let's ride on over there and see if we can tell if you hit anything."

"There's a horse over there," Slocum said.

"Where?" said Jimson.

"I see it," said Buttermilk. "Right over thataway." He pointed, and Jimson squinted into the darkness.

"Let's go slow," Slocum said.

"Yeah," said Jimson.

They eased their mounts forward, riding toward the riderless horse. When they came close to it, they saw the body. Jimson said, "It looks like you hit one of them all right. See who it is, Buttermilk." Buttermilk Smith got off his horse and went over to the body. He knelt down for a closer look. "Damn," he said. "It's ole Merle."

"What?" said Bouvier. "You mean I killed the sheriff?"

Slocum swung down off his Appaloosa and walked over to the body. He knelt across from Buttermilk and struck a match. Then he rolled the body over for a look at the back. He put out the match and stood up, walking back to his horse.

"Charley," he said as he swung back up into the saddle, "were the riders coming at you when you took your shot?"

"Yeah," Bouvier said. "Sure. They were headed right down the trail here."

"Well, you didn't shoot the sheriff," said Slocum, "not unless he was riding the other direction."

"What do you mean?" Jimson said.

"He was shot in the back," Slocum said.

"I didn't shoot no one in the back," said Bouvier. "I didn't give them no warning. I admit that. But I never shot no one in the back. They was headed right this way. All of them."

"Charlie," said Slocum, "you said you saw four riders coming and one horse without a rider."

"Yeah," Bouvier said. "I said that's what it looked like to me. Four riders and one extra horse."

"I think that extra horse was this one right here," Slocum said. "And I think ole Merle here was already dead and slung across that saddle. When Charley shot at them, they dumped the body and took off."

"By God," said Jimson, "I bet you're right."

"It makes sense," said Buttermilk.

"Well, all I know is I didn't shoot no one in the back," Bouvier said.

"We know you didn't," Slocum said. "Did the sheriff have any family around here?"

"He was a loner," said Jimson. "He lived alone, and he never mentioned no family at all that I can recollect. Why you ask that?"

"Because if no one wants the body," Slocum said, "we might as well give him a burying out here. Then just keep our mouths shut. Young and his bunch won't be able to point any fingers in your direction without tipping their own hand."

"Hey, you're right," Jimson said. "But what about his horse?"

"If someone'll ride along with me," Slocum said, "I'll take care of that tonight. Right now, let's load him back up and take him to some other spot. That way if they should come back here to take a look, they won't find anything."

"Go with him, Buttermilk," Jimson said.

"Okay."

"Mr. Jimson," said Slocum.

"Yeah?"

"It looks like you were right this time."

Parley Young sat in a back corner of the Red Ass Saloon with Bowlegs Grigsby, a tough who had worked for him for some time. Young had never gotten close to Grigsby before, but all of a sudden he felt a need. He knew that Goodall and the others would not be back for a while, and he took the opportunity to get Grigsby aside. He bought a bottle and got two glasses, and he poured them both full. Shoving one toward Grigsby, he said, "Drink up, Bowlegs."

Grigsby was curious, but he took the drink. "Thanks," he said.

"Bowlegs," Young said, "I wanted this chance to talk with you in private. I don't want anything I say here to go no further."

"I ain't one to tell no tales," Grigsby said. He took another drink.

"How do you get along with Jerry Goodall?" Young said.

Grigsby shrugged. "He's your foreman," he said. "I work for you, so I do what he tells me to do. That's all."

"He's not a particular friend of yours then?" Young asked.

"I don't reckon I'd have nothing to say to him if we didn't both work for you," Grigsby said.

"I'm going to be straight with you, Bowlegs," said Young. "I made a mistake putting Jerry in that job. He killed Merle. No reason for it. When I jumped him for it, he threatened me. I can't have that, Bowlegs. I put him in that job, but I was wrong. He's not the right man for it. But he's in there, and it's not easy for me to get him out. The man who could, let's say, remove him for me would have the job—and the pay that goes with it. Are you following my drift?"

"It's pretty clear, Mr. Young," Grigsby said. "You can count on me to take care of the situation."

"The sooner the better, Bowlegs," Young said. He poured their glasses full again.

"Mr. Young," Grigsby said, "when I have a job to do, I don't fool around about it. I get it done right now."

"That's what I want to hear," Young said. "Get it done, and you're the foreman."

Back at the Jimson ranch house, Jimson, Slocum, Buttermilk, and Bouvier sat on the porch smoking and drinking whiskey. Both Molly and Felicia also sat on the porch, somewhat removed from the men.

"Mr. Jimson," Buttermilk said, "what's going to happen now without no law around here?"

"There wasn't much before Merle went and got hisself killed," Jimson said. "He sure wasn't doing anything about Parley Young and his gunnies. But I reckon it'll be all out war for sure now. There's no law to hold them back now for sure."

"What's the nearest law?" Slocum asked.

"If I could get to the capital," said Jimson, "I could talk to the governor. He knows me. He'd listen. He'd send a marshal out here. Maybe several deputies with him. He'd take care of the situation all right. But if that Young bunch was to spot me leaving town on the stage, I wouldn't give much for my chances of ever making it to the capital."

"Without any law, we might have to just take things into our own hands and clean that bunch out over there," Slocum said. "You give the word, and I can work it out. We can do that. We can win the war."

"I hate to have to go at it like that," Jimson said. "I wouldn't even consider it if I thought I could get out of here safely and get to the governor."

"Well, there might be a way of making sure that you get through," said Slocum. "We might be able to pull that off, too. Right now, though, I got another chore to take care of. Buttermilk, you want to ride out with me?"

"Sure," Buttermilk said.

"You fixing to do something with ole Merle's horse?" Jimson asked.

"That's right," Slocum said. "Let's go, Buttermilk." He drained his whiskey glass and got up out of his chair. As he headed for the corral, Buttermilk fell in behind him. Soon they were riding away from the ranch house with Slocum riding his Appaloosa and leading the dead sheriff's horse, still saddled. After they had ridden out a ways, Slocum said, "Show me the way to Young's spread."

"The direct way," Buttermilk asked, "or a roundabout way?"

"Roundabout would be best," said Slocum. "We're not looking for a confrontation tonight."

"Just follow me," Buttermilk said. "I'll take you roundabout."

It was two hours later when Buttermilk told Slocum that they were well on Young's ranch. Slocum turned the horse loose. "Now they can accuse us," he said, "and we can accuse them right back. No one'll have any evidence of anything one way or the other. They won't find anything but a stray horse, and they'll find it over here. Now, which way is Young's headquarters?"

Buttermilk pointed southwest. "Thataway," he said. "About another hour's ride."

"Let's go over there," Slocum said. "See if we can pick up a few cows along the way."

Buttermilk wrinkled his nose, but he said, "Okay," and they started riding toward the Young ranch house. When they came across strays, they gathered them up and herded them along. By the time they were halfway there, they had about twenty head. "What the hell are we doing, Slocum?" Buttermilk asked.

"Let's run these cows right smack at the house," Slocum said. "Soon as we get them headed that way real good, we'll turn our own ass around and get the hell out of here. Give them some work to do and something to think about."

Buttermilk grinned. "All right," he said. He took the coiled lariat loose from the saddle and looked at Slocum. "Now?" he said.

Slocum pulled his own rope loose. "Let's run them," he said. Both men whooped and rode at the cattle, swinging their loops. The startled animals bawled and ran, and the two cowboys whooped louder and rode harder, swinging their lariats all the way. Soon they had the small herd in a full stampede. They made sure the stampede was headed right for the Young ranch house, then turned their horses and rode hard away from the scene. At the ranch house, frantic hands fired guns into the air and ran for cover. One corner post supporting the roof over Young's front porch was knocked loose, and the roof sagged. The stampede was over almost as suddenly as it had begun, the small herd having run on through and out into pasture again. When it was finally all over with, the hands looked around some, but they could find no one to blame for the scene. The roof sagged, a wagon in the yard was overturned, and some yard chairs were trampled. One of the men had been knocked down by a cow, but he was only bruised.

"What the hell was that all about?" one of the hands said. "They like to run right over my ass."

"It had to be ole Jimson," said another. "Don't you think? Ain't no one else woulda done that to us on purpose like that."

"I didn't see no one. Just cows."

"But cows has got to have a reason to act crazy like that."

"The boss is going to be real for sure pissed off when

he gets back here after a while and sees this damned mess,"
the first one said. "Let's go on ahead and clean up what we
can before he gets back."

Back at the Red Ass Saloon, Parley Young heard arriving
hoofbeats. It was late, and he didn't think any customers
would be riding up at that hour. Not unless Goodall and
the others were returning from their errand. It would be like
Jerry Goodall to stop off at the saloon rather than report
directly to Young at the ranch house. Of course, Goodall
wouldn't have known that Young had brought Grigsby into
the Red Ass and would be there himself. Young wished
that he had not left the horses out front, but then, he hadn't
been expecting Goodall either. He moved quickly to the
front window and peered out. It was Goodall, all right, and
his three closest cronies. Young hurried back to his chair.

"That's Jerry and those other three coming right now,"
he said. "Don't let on that anything's out of the ordinary."

"You don't have to worry about me," Grigsby said, but
he stood up as he was talking. Walking toward the front
door, he pulled his six-gun and checked it. He stepped to
the left side of the door and pressed his back against the
wall and waited. Young began to sweat. He could hear the
voices of Goodall and the others outside, and he could hear
the footsteps on the board sidewalk. In another instant, the
batwing doors were thrown open, and Jerry Goodall
stepped in. He was talking in a loud voice over his shoulder
to the men who were following him. He took only one long
step into the Red Ass when Grigsby raised his six-gun and
pulled the trigger.

Young watched, fascinated, as a look of total shock came
over Goodall's face. The scarface flinched, staggered forward a couple of steps, then collapsed onto the floor.
Snider, Tallman, and Orwig stepped inside. Snider was
holding a bandanna to his hurt shoulder. All three men
stopped and looked unbelieving at the body of Goodall
there in front of them. They turned toward Grigsby and
made motions as if they would go for their guns, but they
all hesitated, unsure. Grigsby's gun was out and ready, and

they could see their boss, Young, just sitting there at a table and watching.

"Don't try it, boys," Grigsby said.

They moved their hands away from the gun butts, and then they looked over at Young still seated at the table. "Listen to him, boys," Young said. "He's your new foreman. Drag ole Jerry out of here, and then come on over and sit down with me. We'll all have us a drink together, and I'll explain everything to you."

As Orwig and Tallman bent to grab hold of Goodall's remains and drag them out the front door, Snider stepped toward Young with a pitiful look on his face, and he spoke in a whiny voice.

"Mr. Young, sir," he said, "I been hurt bad. I need me a doctor."

7

Felicia was taking a break on the front porch of the Jimson ranch house when Buttermilk Smith came walking by. She said good morning to him, and he stopped and doffed his hat. "Morning, ma'am," he said.

"You want a cup of coffee?" she asked him. "I wouldn't mind some company. You got time?"

"Well, yes, ma'am," Buttermilk said. "I reckon I do. That is, if you're sure it would be all right."

"Come on up and have a chair," she said. "I'll fetch us out some coffee."

Buttermilk climbed up onto the porch and took a seat as Felicia went into the house. In a short while, she returned with two cups of coffee, and she gave one to Buttermilk. He thanked her kindly and took a tentative sip.

"Um, that's nice and hot," he said.

"Fresh brewed," Felicia said.

"Miss," he began, but Felicia stopped him.

"Please," she said, "call me Felicia."

"Well, all right," he said. "Well, ma'am, uh, Felicia, I sure am glad that ole Slocum brought you out here out of that place in town."

"Why, Buttermilk?" she asked him.

"Well," he said, "it's just nice having you out here, I guess."

"Is that all?"

"No, I guess it ain't," he said. "I just never did like seeing you in there. You're too pretty and too nice for—well, for that."

Felicia blushed. "How come you never came to see me, Buttermilk?" she asked.

"I couldn't bring myself to," he said. "I thought about it lots of times, but I just couldn't. Not like that. Not you. Anyhow, I'm glad you're here—even if you did come with Slocum."

"Thank you," she said, trying to figure out just what to make of Buttermilk's words.

"When this trouble's all over," he said, "you going to ride on out of here with him?"

"With Slocum?" she asked.

"Yeah," he said. "You going to ride on out with Slocum?"

"In the first place," she said, "he's never asked me. I don't think he's the type, Buttermilk. He's the love 'em and leave 'em type, you know? He's a wanderer and a loner. Shoot, I even heard him call himself a saddle bum once."

"Oh, well, I just thought that—"

"Thought what?" she said.

"Sure is good coffee, Felicia," he said. "You reckon I could have me another cup?"

Just then Slocum and Jimson came out of the house. "Buttermilk," Jimson said, "I'm glad you're here. We just made some plans. I want you to go tell some of the boys to start driving all our cows back east of the house. That's a precaution in case Young's bunch decides to come at us again. We get all the cattle back there behind us, then we'll move our guards back closer to the house. Once you get the boys going, come back here. Bring three horses; Slocum's and one each for you and me. We're going into town."

"Right away, Mr. Jimson," Buttermilk said. He tipped

his hat to Felicia. "Thanks for the coffee," he said, "and the visit."

Young and Grigsby were stepping out of the Red Ass when they saw Jimson, Slocum, and Buttermilk riding into Harleyville. Young put out an arm to halt Grigsby's progress. The two men stepped back inside the doorway and watched.

"That's Slocum," said Young. "We thought he'd left these parts. Wonder where they're going?"

"Looks to me like they're headed for the stage office," Grigsby said.

"Yeah," said Young. "You're right."

As they watched, Jimson and the other two tied their horses outside the stage office and went inside.

"What the hell is that son of a bitch up to?" Young said, musing rather than expecting an answer.

"Soon as they leave, I can go find out," Grigsby said, "if you want me to."

"Yeah," Young said. "You do that."

They watched for a few more minutes. Then the three from Jimson's came back out of the stage office, mounted up again, and rode back toward the Red Ass. In another moment, Young said, "Damn. They're coming right over here. Go on out the back door, Bowlegs. Hurry up."

Grigsby hurried through the room and out the back, and Young went to his table at the far end of the room. He sat down to wait. Jimson came in, followed by Slocum and Buttermilk. Spotting Young, Jimson stopped. "I ain't sure about the company in here, boys," he said.

"We got as much right as he has," Slocum said.

"You're right," said Jimson. He stepped up to the bar and ordered three cold beers. The three men took their beers and went to a table and sat down. Slocum took out a cigar and lit it. Then Young stood up and walked boldly over to their table.

"Well," he said, "you found yourself a job around here after all, Slocum. We thought you'd left these parts for good."

"I don't have a job," Slocum said. "I'm just hanging around—visiting friends."

"Is that right?" Young said.

"That's right," said Slocum, "and what made you think I'd left these parts?"

"Oh, we just hadn't seen you around," Young said. "You checked out of the hotel and took your horse out of the stable. We didn't see you after that. Not till just now."

"What else do you know about the day I left the hotel?" Slocum asked him.

"Oh, nothing much," Young said.

"You don't know anything about a reception committee that was waiting for me at the stable?"

"Seems like I did hear something about that," said Young. "You seem to be doing all right now though."

"It was four men that work for you," said Slocum. "The main one was called Goodall. Scar-faced son of a bitch."

"Oh, Jerry?" Young said. "I'll be damned. He always was one to take something on himself without asking for my opinion. He went and got himself killed the other day. You hear about that? It was right in here, too."

"Who killed him?" Jimson asked.

"Damned if I know," said Young. "I wasn't here. No one seems to have seen who it was did the shooting. I'd have Merle investigating, but Merle seems to have disappeared. I can't imagine what's become of him."

"I can imagine," said Jimson.

Just then Bowlegs Grigsby came walking in the front door. He stepped up beside his boss and stood staring at Jimson and the others.

"Bowlegs," said Young, "you know these gentlemen here?"

"All but that one," Grigsby said, thrusting a chin toward Slocum.

"Well," said Young, "that there is Mr. John Slocum. He's a gunfighter that ole Carl here has got hanging around his place."

"A gunfighter, huh?" Grigsby said. "I don't think we need no gunfighters hanging around here, Boss, do you?"

"Hell, Bowlegs," said Young, "it's none of my business who hangs out at Jimson's spread. He could have Billy the Kid out there for all I care."

"You thinking about running me out, Bowlegs?" Slocum said. " 'Cause if you are, you might like to know that I have my Colt under the table trained right on your balls."

Grigsby turned a little pale at that thought. "I'm just talking," he said. "For now."

"If you want more than talk," Slocum said, "why wait? We can get it over with right now. Just say the word, chicken shit."

Grigsby trembled with anger, but Young laughed. He put a hand on Grigsby's shoulder.

"Now, now," he said, "we didn't come in here for no fight. Let's go, Bowlegs. These boys don't seem to be in a friendly mood just now."

Young and Grigsby headed for the door.

"I wish you had gone ahead and blowed his balls off, Slocum," Jimson said.

"Seems to me," said Slocum, "you were the one who wanted to do things according to the law."

"Yeah," Jimson said, "you're right. I guess I really didn't mean that. Not much, I didn't. Say, were you really holding your Colt ready under the table?"

Slocum raised his hands up above the tabletop. They were both empty.

"You son of a bitch," said Buttermilk. "What if he'd called your bluff?"

"If he'd killed me," Slocum said, "I expect you'd have done me the favor of killing him."

"Well, yeah, I would have," Buttermilk said.

Outside at the hitch rail, Grigsby spoke low to Young.

"That Slocum's a bad one," he said. "I'll be glad when you're ready for me to kill him. I'll enjoy that one."

"The time will come, Bowlegs," Young said. "Did you find anything out at the station?"

"Old man Jimson bought hisself a ticket to the capital on the next stage. He'll be leaving tomorrow noon."

"He's a pal of the governor's," Young said. "It's a sure bet that's where he's going. To see the governor. And he'll do plenty of talking, too. Bowlegs, we can't afford to let him get there. You get my meaning?"

"He'll never reach the capital alive," Grigsby said. "You can count on me."

Young and Grigsby mounted their horses and rode out of town.

In the Red Ass, Slocum sipped a whiskey. He was thinking that Grigsby had come in at an interesting time. He downed the whiskey and stood up. "I'll be right back," he said. Without another word of explanation, he walked out the front door. He made his way to the stage office and walked in.

"Can I help you?" asked the little man behind the counter.

"Mr. Jimson just bought a ticket," Slocum said.

"Yes," the little man said. "I know. I sold it to him."

"Did Bowlegs Grigsby come in here right after that?" Slocum asked.

"Well, now, let me see," the man mumbled.

"Don't play any games with me, you little shit," said Slocum. "Did Grigsby come in here?"

"Yes," the man said, "he did."

"What for?"

"He wanted to know where Mr. Jimson was going—and when."

"And you told him?"

"Well, yes. I did."

The little man was trembling by this time.

"Thanks," Slocum said. "That's all I wanted to know." He turned and left the office.

In a few more minutes, Slocum, Buttermilk, and Jimson were riding back toward Jimson's ranch, but Jimson had bought a bottle to take along with them on the ride. He took himself a long drink, then passed the bottle to Slocum. As Slocum tipped it back, Jimson burst into song, some

Irish ditty that Slocum did not recognize. Slocum passed the bottle to Buttermilk. By the time they reached the ranch, they were all more than a bit drunk. Jimson was a strange combination of silly and belligerent. Buttermilk was loud and silly. Slocum was quiet, slow, and staggering.

At the ranch house, Jimson roared out for someone, and the call was answered by Charley Bouvier. "Take care of our horses, Charley," Jimson said. "We're too drunk. We might hurt them." Buttermilk laughed and fell back on the porch. Slocum carefully took himself up to his favorite chair on the porch, sat, extracted a cigar from his pocket, then a match, struck the match, and lit the cigar. Buttermilk rolled over to watch him as if the whole process was fascinating.

"You want one of these, Buttermilk?" Slocum asked.

"Yeah," Buttermilk said. "Thanks."

Slocum handed Buttermilk a cigar and then a match, and Buttermilk worked at appearing very sophisticated while lighting up. Jimson, sure at last that Bouvier would take care of all three horses, climbed up onto the porch and fell into a chair. "You got another one of them things, Slocum?" he asked.

"Sure," Slocum said. He gave a cigar and a match to Jimson. Jimson fired his up.

"Goddamn it," he said. "I wish that son of a bitch Young and his snarly dog Grigsby would ride up here right now. Now I'm in the mood for killing. I'd shoot them both down like dogs. Worse. I'd shoot them like prairie dogs or coyotes or snakes. That's what I'd do. I'd kill the bastards dead. I would."

"Being drunk ain't the best time for killing," Slocum said.

"Bullshit," said Jimson. "What's better?"

"Sober," Slocum said. "When you can see straight and shoot straight. And if you get lucky and do kill someone when you're drunk, you might be sorry for it when you sober up."

"Not if it was Young and Grigsby and them I wouldn't," Jimson said.

Charley Bouvier came walking back from the corral just as Jimson passed out, his chin dropping to his chest. "Boss have a pretty good time tonight?" Bouvier asked.

"You might say that, Charley," Slocum said. "You want to help us get him inside?"

"Sure," said Bouvier.

They took care of Jimson, and when they returned to their seats on the porch, the two ladies came out with them to sit for a while. Buttermilk offered Bouvier a drink, but Bouvier refused it. "Good," said Slocum, "someone besides the ladies needs to keep a clear head tonight."

"That's kind of what I was thinking," Bouvier said.

"Did Carl get his ticket to the capital?" Molly asked.

"Yes, ma'am," Slocum said. "He did. The stage leaves tomorrow at noon."

"I'll see that he's ready to go," said Molly. She stood up, said her good nights, and went back inside. Felicia stayed on the porch with the men.

"Charley," said Slocum, "you want to have a rig ready to take Mr. Jimson into town in the morning?"

"I'll have it ready to go," Bouvier said. "I'll get him there in plenty of time."

"Good," said Slocum. "Me and ole Buttermilk here have got us another chore to look after so we won't be available."

Buttermilk looked at Slocum with a puzzled expression. "What's that?" he said. "What have we got to do in the morning?"

"We'll talk about it later," Slocum said. "Just now, I ain't fit for straight talk, and you ain't fit to listen."

Buttermilk laughed out loud as if Slocum had just told a real funny joke. Then he took another drink from the bottle. He stretched his arm, reaching the bottle toward Slocum.

"No, thanks," Slocum said. "I've had enough."

Buttermilk suddenly felt foolish. He glanced at Felicia. The boss was in bed, passed out, Slocum had stopped drinking, and Charley Bouvier was sober. Buttermilk had just taken another drink, and he knew that he was already silly drunk. And just over there almost beside him was Felicia, the last person in the world he wanted to look foolish around. He plugged the bottle and put it on the ground in front of the porch. "Well," he said, "I reckon I have, too. Had enough, that is. So I better cut it out."

Bouvier stood up. "It's about time to change the guards," he said. "I better go make sure the boys are all ready."

"We got us a big day tomorrow, Buttermilk," Slocum said. "I'm going to turn in. You ought to do the same."

He went into the house, leaving Buttermilk and Felicia alone on the porch. They sat for a moment in silence.

"I—uh—I reckon he's right," Buttermilk said. "I reckon I ought to go turn in, too."

"What's this big day you and Slocum have tomorrow?" Felicia asked him.

"I sure don't know," Buttermilk said. "He never told me. So I reckon I'll just have to be ready for any ole thing he comes up with. The boss is taking the stage to the capital tomorrow, but I don't know what me and Slocum is going to do."

"Well, whatever it is," Felicia said, "be careful."

Buttermilk stood up, hat in hand. He faced Felicia with his head hanging, more than a little ashamed of himself.

"Thank you for your concern, Miss Felicia," he said, "and I sure do want to apologize to you for my disgraceful condition here this evening."

"You don't have to apologize, Buttermilk," she said. "You just had a few drinks is all. You were with Slocum and Mr. Jimson, and you all had a few drinks. It's all right."

"Thank you again," he said.

"Nonsense," she said, and she stood up and walked over toward him. He was standing on the ground, and she was on the porch. She looked down at him. His head was still hanging. She moved down the steps to stand just in front of him, and she put a hand on his chin and raised his head. They looked into each other's eyes. Buttermilk felt his heart pound in his chest. He gripped his hat hard by its brim. Felicia put a hand on each of his cheeks and pulled his face toward hers. She kissed him on the lips.

"Good night, Buttermilk," she said. She turned and went

back up onto the porch and on inside the house. Buttermilk stood for a moment alone, feeling dumbstruck. He could hardly believe what had just happened. Suddenly he flung his hat high into the air, let out a wild cowboy whoop, and turned and ran toward the bunkhouse. Along the way, he tripped and fell. He got up, gave another whoop, and continued on his way.

8

Slocum found Buttermilk right after breakfast the next morning, and he drew him off to one side for a private talk. Buttermilk had gotten up with a slight hangover, but the good meal had just about taken care of that little problem. "What is it, Slocum?" he asked.

"Buttermilk," Slocum said, "you know that Mr. Jimson is headed off for the capital today on that noon stage."

"Sure," said Buttermilk, "I know that. He leaves on the noon stage. It was all fixed up yesterday. I was in town with you, you know."

"You know too that Young knows that?" Slocum said.

"No," Buttermilk said. "How do you know?"

"Remember when I left you and Mr. Jimson last night in the saloon?" Slocum asked.

"Yeah. I figured you had to go take a piss or something."

"I went down to the stage office," Slocum said. "The man there admitted to me that Grigsby had been in there just after Mr. Jimson and asked where he was going and when. The man told him."

"Why, the little chicken shit," Buttermilk said.

"That's not important," said Slocum. "What is important is that Young and Grigsby know that Jimson's going to be

71

on that stage. Now, we know why the boss is going to the capital, and I expect that Young will figure it all out without straining his brain too much."

"Yeah. I reckon he will," Buttermilk agreed. "You s'pose he'll try to stop that stage?"

"What would you do in his place?"

"What're we going to do about it, Slocum?"

"I figured you and me would dog that stage for a while and make sure that it gets well on its way," Slocum said. "We could run into trouble. In fact, I expect that we will. Are you up for that kind of work?"

Buttermilk turned away from Slocum for a moment. When he turned back, his face was set grim. "If I was to tell you my real name," he said, "you'd know me. And you'd know that I was more than ready for that kind of work. I come here to work for Mr. Jimson to put all that behind me. No one knows who I really am, and no one knows what has become of that feller I used to be. But I'm your man, Slocum. Let's see it done."

Slocum tried to take in just what Buttermilk had confided in him just then. Was it a secret past? And did it have something to do with gunfighting and killing?

"You afraid you might tip your hand like this?" Slocum asked.

Buttermilk shook his head. "I ain't going to do no show-boating," he said. "That don't worry me none. Mr. Jimson is a good boss—a good man. I work for him, and I mean to see that he gets through this all right."

"All right," Slocum said. "Have yourself ready. When Charley starts to drive Mr. Jimson to town, we'll trail along."

It came to Slocum in just a few minutes that he knew who Buttermilk Smith really was. There had been a young gunfighter with a mean reputation down along the Rio Grande a few years ago. He couldn't have been more than eighteen years old, and folks had been comparing him to Billy the Kid. Of course, they were actually comparing him to the Billy the Kid legend. Slocum knew that the real Billy had been a backshooter, and this other kid, well, he was a hell of a gunfighter. Slocum had heard enough about him from reliable sources to know that. He was known as the Rock Port Kid, and he was much feared. But then, he had just disappeared. Dropped out of sight. So, Slocum thought, Buttermilk Smith must be the Rock Port Kid. He resolved, though, to keep that speculation to himself.

The stage rolled out of Harleyville just on time, and Carl Jimson was on it. The only person from the Jimson ranch in town to see him off was Charley Bouvier, who had driven him to town. As the stage rumbled off toward the capital, beginning a two-day trip, Bouvier turned the rig around and headed back toward the ranch. Jimson settled back for a long ride. He was the only passenger on the stage. Up on the box, his old friend Amos Tuttle was driving. Elkhide Rawlins was riding shotgun. Jimson was not sure just what Governor Davis would do, but he knew that the governor would see him and listen to him, and he was almost as sure that he would do something about it. He was anxious to reach the capital and get to the governor's office. He rehearsed the speech he would make over and over again in his head.

Bowlegs Grigsby sat on his horse atop a rise watching the road below. With him were Jody Tallman and Red Orwig. "What're your plans, Bowlegs?" Orwig asked.

"Stop the stage," said Grigsby. "Kill them all."

"Kill them all?" said Tallman.

"We don't want no witnesses," Grigsby explained.

The stage rolled into sight about then, and Grigsby told Orwig, "Take out your rifle and knock off the driver."

Orwig pulled a Henry out of the scabbard on the left side of his saddle. He cranked a shell into the chamber and raised the rifle to his shoulder. He waited for the stage to get within good range. About the time he had a good bead on the driver and was about to pull the trigger, he noticed that the shotgun guard had a rifle trained on him. "Damn," he said, and he snapped off a quick shot, but he knew that it went wild. Rawlins's shot popped just an instant after

Orwig's, and it took the hat off Orwig's head. Grigsby
jerked out his revolver and kicked his horse in the sides.
"Let's go get them," he shouted. He raced toward the stage,
Orwig and Tallman right behind him.

Tuttle whipped up the horses, and Rawlins fired another
shot, but with the stage jouncing so, it went wild. Grigsby
and the others were moving fast down the incline toward
the road, when they saw two riders coming down the slope
on the other side. In another instant, they saw that the two
riders were shooting at them. Then Tallman roared out in
pain and slowed his mount. A slug had torn into his right
elbow from the front, and his right arm dangled bloody and
useless.

"It's that goddamned Slocum," Grigsby yelled. "Get
him."

A bullet from Buttermilk's six-gun tore into Grigsby's
left foot just then. It passed through the foot and wounded
the horse. The horse went down, and Grigsby somehow
managed to get to his feet. Hopping and limping, he
shouted at Orwig. "Pick me up. Pick me up, damn it."

"I'm getting out of here," Orwig said, spurring his horse
around to make a speedy retreat. Tallman rode up beside
Grigsby, and Grigsby struggled up on the horse behind
Tallman. Blood dripping from Tallman's arm and Grigsby's
foot, they hurried after Orwig. Slocum and Buttermilk fired
a few shots after them just to hurry them along their way.
The stage was well down the road by this time. Slocum
pulled up his big Appaloosa, and Buttermilk rode up beside
him and stopped.

"I reckon we spoiled their plans," Buttermilk said.

"For now," Slocum said. "But they won't quit. I'd feel
a whole lot better about Mr. Jimson if you were to trail that
stage all the way to the capital and back."

Buttermilk grinned. "I think that's a hell of a good idea,"
he said.

"It's two days there and two days back," Slocum said.
"We didn't pack any trail food. Are there places enough
along the way to stop and eat?"

"Yeah," Buttermilk said. "There's a plenty."

"You got enough cash on you?"

"I still got most of my last pay," Buttermilk said. "Don't worry about me. I'll do just fine. See you in a few days, pardner."

Buttermilk turned his horse to ride after the stage. Slocum sat and watched him ride off for a moment. Then he rode after Grigsby, Tallman, and Orwig. It wasn't long before he caught up with the two riding double. Orwig was long gone. When Grigsby became aware of the rider behind them, he poked Tallman in the back. "Slocum's coming," he said.

"We can't get away from him riding double like this," said Tallman. "And we're both hurt. What'll we do?"

"Ride over to that clump of boulders over there," Grigsby said. "Hurry."

Slocum saw them ride behind the rocks and dismount. He rode easy, and he stopped just out of range of their six-guns. A good rifle shot might hit him, but he knew they were both hurt. He pulled his own rifle out of its scabbard and cranked a shell into the chamber. "You two," he shouted.

"What do you want?" Grigsby answered.

"I can hold you behind those rocks long enough for you to bleed to death," Slocum said, "or you can toss out your guns and come out."

"You'll kill us," Grigsby said.

"Not if you do what I say," said Slocum. "Anyhow, what's the difference? Stay there and bleed, or take my word that I won't kill you and come on out."

Behind the rocks, Tallman turned to Grigsby. "He's right," he said. "We stay here, we'll bleed to death. I'm still bleeding like a stuck pig."

"Shut up," Grigsby said. "We could pick him off with a rifle shot. Then we'd each one have us a horse. We could get into town to the doc before we bleed to death."

"I can't shoot no rifle," said Tallman. "My arm's busted. It hurts like hell, too."

"My foot hurts like hell, too," Grigsby said, "but I can

damn sure shoot a rifle. Go get yours offa your horse. Hurry it up."

Tallman, ducking low, went back to his horse and pulled the rifle loose with his good arm. He sneaked back to Grigsby's side and handed the rifle to Grigsby. Grigsby chambered a shell and took aim over the rocks. Just then, Slocum fired. His lead hit the rock just in front of Grigsby, peppering Grigsby's face with tiny rock shards, glancing up and tearing off Grigsby's right thumb. Grigsby howled. He dropped the rifle. "Give it up, Bowlegs," Tallman said in a desperate voice.

"Fuck you, chicken shit," Grigsby said.

Tallman pulled out his six-gun with his good hand and bashed Grigsby in the back of the head. Grigsby slumped, and Orwig hit him again and again. He kept hitting until the body was lifeless and the back of the head was like mush. Then he flung the six-gun out over the rocks. He pulled Grigsby's revolver out of the holster at the dead man's side and flung it. Then he tossed the Winchester. He stood up waving his good arm.

"I done it," he yelled. "I tossed out all our guns. Don't shoot."

"Where's your pardner?" Slocum asked.

"Dead," said Tallman. "He wouldn't quit, and I bashed in his head."

"You wouldn't lie to me, would you?" Slocum asked.

"No, hell no," said Tallman. "I swear to God."

"I don't think that oath's worth much either," Slocum said. "If he's back there dead, grab hold of him and drag him out where I can see."

Tallman took a grip on the dead Grigsby's collar and started dragging. It was slow and tough work. He had only one arm to use, and he was feeling weak from loss of blood. He dragged the body, and he started crying from fright and from pain. When Slocum got a good look and was convinced of the truth of Tallman's statement, he rode forward. Closer, he saw the bashed-in head.

"Damn," he said, "you really took care of him."

"He was trying to get me killed," Tallman whimpered.

"Mister, I done what you said, and I'm bleeding to death here."

Slocum dismounted and walked toward Tallman.

"Sit down," he said. "I'll do what I can. Then you can ride on into town to see the doc. When he's finished with you, I want you to get out of this country for good. Understand?"

"I'll get as far from here as I can," Tallman said. "I promise you that. I'll get way away."

Slocum patched Tallman's arm the best he could. The bleeding was stopped. He gave Tallman some water, and he waited a few minutes. At last he got up to leave. He took the three guns Tallman had tossed out. Mounting his horse, he looked down at the pitiful wretch on the ground.

"You can make it into town all right," he said. "I don't ever want to see you again."

"You won't, mister," said Tallman. "I guarantee it. You won't never see me again."

Slocum rode off without looking back. He was thinking that he could easily have killed the worthless shit back there, but really, that might have been too merciful. He could tell that the man's arm was useless. It would never be good again. He might even lose it to amputation. And where would a one-armed bully find any work? Leaving him alive might have been the worst punishment he could inflict on the son of bitch.

Orwig rode an exhausted horse up to the ranch headquarters at Young's place. He practically jumped out of the saddle, raced up onto the porch, and barged in through the front door without knocking. Young jumped up, surprised, from behind his big desk. "What the hell?" he said.

"Boss," said Orwig, panting, "Slocum met us out there. Slocum and that cowboy they call Buttermilk. They got Bowlegs and Jody. I'm lucky I got away. Boss, that Slocum's a professional gunfighter, and Buttermilk—I never seen him in action before—but he's damn near as good."

"Shit," said Young. "So the stage got through?"

"Damn right it got through," Orwig said. "What the hell

could I do? Bowlegs and Jody both out of commission and just me against them two gunmen? I couldn't do nothing but just get away. That's all."

"Are Bowlegs and Jody both killed?" Young asked.

"I bet they are by now," Orwig said. "Hell, they was both hit bad, and Bowlegs's horse was down. They couldn't have got very far, not the way they was hit."

Young paced the floor in deep thought.

"Boss," Orwig said, "what're we going to do? We can't stop ole Jimson now. That stage is long gone. And we can't fight them two gunfighters neither. We're licked, Boss."

"Shut up," Young said. "I've got me an ace or two up my sleeve yet. We ain't licked, and don't let me hear you say it again."

"Well then, what'll we do?"

"Just sit tight," Young said. "Put out guards so they can't ride in and surprise us like they did with that little stampede a while back."

"Yeah, but when ole Jimson comes back from the capital," Orwig said, "no telling who he'll be bringing with him. Troops maybe or a posse or something."

"Stop thinking," said Young. "It don't become you. If Jimson comes back with any help, likely it'll be just one marshal. That's all. And we'll be ready for him, and for Buttermilk and Slocum. Here. Take a look at this."

He picked up a paper from off the top of his desk and handed it to Orwig. Orwig took it and looked at it with a blank expression on his face.

"Aw, hell, Boss," he said, "I can't read."

Young jerked the paper back from Orwig. "This is a letter," he said. "A letter I received in response to one that I wrote. It's from Aaron Parsons. That name mean anything to you?"

"Aaron Parsons," Orwig mused, wrinkling his face in thought. "Say, ain't he the one they call One Shot? He always hits a man right between the eyes."

"That's the one," Young said.

"Well, how come you to write a letter to him?" Orwig asked. "You got him coming here? What's he say?"

"Aaron Parsons, One Shot, will be here just any day now," Young said. "He can take care of Slocum and Buttermilk and anyone else that Jimson brings back from the capital with him. Parsons will be taking over our operation here as soon as he arrives. We got nothing else to worry about."

Orwig wrinkled his brow and walked away from Young. Then he turned back. "I don't know," he said. "I mean, I'm sure you're right about ole One Shot. From what I hear, he can damn sure do all that what you said he can do. But if the governor sends a man down here, and that man gets killed, won't he just send more? How we going to get away with that?"

"If everyone on the other side is dead," Young said, "we'll be the only witnesses left alive to tell the tale. They'll have to take our word for how it happened. We'll have a good story ready telling how it was Carl Jimson who started all the trouble and killed Merle. Ever' one of us will tell the same thing. They won't have no choice but to accept what we say. Whether they like it or not."

When Slocum rode back to the ranch alone, an obviously worried Felicia asked him about Buttermilk. Slocum told her where Buttermilk had gone and why. She was some relieved, but not completely. He could tell that she was overly concerned about the young cowhand. *She's interested in him,* Slocum thought. *I guess I better step aside and let her have at him. Be best for both of them.*

Molly came out of the house, too, very much concerned about the safety of her husband. Slocum told her the whole tale. He told both women how the Young gunnies had tried to stop the stage but had been stopped themselves instead.

"Don't worry. The stage and everyone on it is on its way to the capital," he said. "There's no one following it either. Not anymore. No one except for Buttermilk. I sent him along to make sure it stays safe, and from what I saw of him in action today, believe me, ladies, he can take care of himself and maybe the rest of us all at the same time."

"Well," Molly said, "I'll sure be glad when Carl's back home safe."

"He will be," Slocum said. "And we'll get this whole mess with Young all cleared up."

"Well then," Molly said, "if he was here right now, he'd offer you a drink. Shall I go get the bottle?"

"Well, ma'am," Slocum said, "do you maybe have just a little snort now and then yourself?"

"It's been known to happen," Molly said.

"In that case, ma'am," he said, "I'd be just real pleased to have a drink with you."

9

Buck Snider walked into the big ranch house on the Young spread, hat in hand. Parley Young was sitting behind his big desk. He looked up. "Come on in, Buck," he said. Snider walked uncertainly over to the desk. He had never been called into the big house before. "Sit down," Young said. Snider sat in the straight chair across the desk from Young. "Red said you wanted to see me, Boss," he said.

"How's that bullet wound healing?" Young asked.

"I'm most near good as new," said Snider. "Just a little stiff is all."

"Then you can ride all right?"

"Aw, hell, yes," said Snider. "I can ride just fine."

"Does ole Carl Jimson know you?" Young asked. "Would he recognize you if he was to see you?"

"Well," said Snider, "I ain't never really met him. He might coulda saw me around town or something. I don't know. I ain't for real sure, but I kinda think that he wouldn't know me if he was to look me in the face."

"That'll have to do then," said Young. "I want you to take a good horse and ride over to the capital. Ole Jimson's gone over there on the stage to talk to the governor, and they're old pards. I want you to hang around there and see what you can find out. Then whenever he gets on the stage to head on back over thisaway, I want you to mount up and beat that damn stage back over here and give me a full report. You got that?"

"Yes sir," said Snider. "I can take keer a that."

Young handed Snider a roll of bills.

"Here's for your expenses," he said. "Now get moving."

Carl Jimson knew that the stage had been attacked, and he knew that the attackers had been driven off, almost for sure by Slocum. Slocum had almost certainly had some help, but it could have been any one or more of his young ranch hands. Jouncing along in the stage, Jimson thought about his first reaction to Slocum, and he thought about how fortunate he was to have Slocum around. Jimson wasn't afraid of Parley Young and his gang, but having Slocum around sure did ease his mind. He had to admit it. He vowed silently to be a little more careful in the future about making snap judgments and generalizations.

He figured that he and his boys could probably beat Young's outfit in a straight-out, fair fight, if it came to that. Especially with Slocum running the fight for his side. But he didn't want to do it that way. There were laws, and Jimson was one who liked to stay within the law. If he was to get all his boys together with Slocum in charge and just attack the Young place and wipe them out, why, the way he looked at it, he wouldn't be any better than Parley Young. At least, that's the way he felt about it. This trip to the governor was important. He had to talk to him and let him know how things were with Parley Young. He had to get, if not the governor's help, then at least the governor's sanction for his own actions.

He wasn't surprised that Young had tried to stop him, but he was even less surprised that Slocum had stopped Young. He wondered what would happen around the ranch in his absence. He hated leaving the place during this time of trouble, but he was the only one who could talk to his old friend Bob Davis about this situation. He was really counting on Slocum to keep the wolves away while he met with Governor Davis. He knew that he would be gone at least five days. A lot could happen in five days.

Buttermilk rode alert. He kept the stagecoach mostly in sight, but he kept himself back far enough that he wouldn't be spotted. At the same time, he watched around on all sides just in case any of Young's bunch should make a second try at stopping his boss from getting through to the capital. Even with all this in mind, his brain still had time to wander back to the ranch and Felicia. Buttermilk thought that Felicia was the most lovely creature he had ever set eyes on in his whole life. He knew how she had been making her living, of course. That didn't bother him. He wouldn't worry over her past, if she wouldn't worry about his. The main thing was keeping her from going back to that life.

He knew that he would have to tell her about the Rock Port Kid, and he hoped that the knowledge would not make any difference to her in the way she felt about him. But it did worry him some. After all, he had been a killer with a notorious reputation. She might not like that. He tried to decide just when and how he should tell her, and he thought that he might best wait until he was sure how she felt about him. But then, that wouldn't be fair, he decided. He ought to tell her right away. Then if his past was repugnant to her, she could brush him aside without having gotten herself too deeply involved. Yes, he decided, that was the thing to do. He would tell her all about it the first chance he got.

Not wanting to lord it over the cowhands in the absence of their boss, Slocum dealt with Charley Bouvier. He let Bouvier give the orders. He kept the guards out, and he saw to it that the cattle were all moved to pastures east of the ranch house. There would be no more killing of Jimson cows. And Slocum made the rounds each night. He rode out to check on the sentries, and he made further rounds. After all, sentries couldn't see everything everywhere. Things were quiet though. Slocum figured it to be the calm before the storm.

He tried to move his things out to the bunkhouse in the absence of Carl Jimson, but Molly wouldn't hear of it. "You're a guest in this house," she said. "Why, Carl would raise the roof on me if he was to come home and find you moved out. You'll stay right where you are."

It was morning of the second day. Jimson would be starting the second and last leg of his journey to the capital. Buttermilk would still be dogging the trail of the stage. The day before had been quiet and uneventful. Molly came out of the house to find Slocum on the porch. She said good morning, then began looking around. Slocum stood up.

"Can I help you?" he said.

"Oh, I was just looking to see if I could find Charley or one of the boys," Molly said. "I need a few things from town, and I thought I'd get someone to hitch up the buggy and drive me in."

"How about you just draw me up a list and let me see to it?" Slocum said. "I'd feel better if you just stayed right here."

"Well, all right," she said. She went back in the house, and in a few minutes came back and handed the list to Slocum. He looked it over, then tucked it into his pocket.

"I'll take care of this right away," he said. He headed over toward the corral and barn, and on the way he met Bouvier. "Charley," he said, "can you get a rig hitched up for me? Miz Jimson needs some stuff from town."

"I'll hitch it up for you and ride in with you," Bouvier said.

"You ought to stay here and look after things," Slocum said.

"I got the boys all busy," Bouvier said. "They won't even miss me."

"Well, all right then," Slocum said. "Let's get it done."

In Harleyville, they stopped in front of the general store. Slocum went inside, but Bouvier stood on the board sidewalk and rolled himself a cigarette. He struck a match on the wall and lit up. He stood there watching as four cowhands from the Young place rode into town, hitched their horses to the rail in front of the saloon, and went inside. Bouvier looked around. He saw a boy, maybe twelve years old, playing with a dog a couple of doors down. He strolled over and sat down beside the boy.

"Nice-looking dog you got there," Bouvier said.

"It ain't my dog," the boy said.

Bouvier looked at the four Young horses across the street. He pulled a coin out of his shirt pocket. "How'd you like to make a dollar?" he asked the boy.

"A whole dollar?" the boy said. "Who do I have to kill?"

Bouvier chuckled. "It ain't that bad," he said. He pulled a jackknife out of his pocket, opened it up, and handed it to the boy. "See them four horses over there?" he said.

"Sure I see them," the boy said.

"Well, if you was to sneak over there and just sort of slice them four cinch straps with this here knife," Bouvier said, "you could have this here dollar and the knife. But you'd have to be pretty sneaky and not get yourself caught. Cut them all the way through. It'll be a good joke on them cowboys."

"Hell," the boy said, "I can do it."

Bouvier handed the boy the dollar, and the boy jumped up and ran across the street. Bouvier stood up and strolled back to his spot in front of the general store. He puffed on his cigarette and watched. The boy stood in front of the saloon for a moment, looking up and down the street. Then he moved casually down to the hitch rail. He ducked under the rail to stand between two horses. Bouvier could not see what the boy was doing, but in another moment, he did see the boy duck again and move over between the other two horses. Then the boy strolled back up onto the sidewalk, trying his best to look innocent. He looked over at Bouvier and made a sign, then strolled off grinning. Bouvier took a final puff on his cigarette, threw the butt into the street, and went into the general store to join Slocum there.

Slocum was about done with the shopping. Bouvier settled the bill with the storekeeper, then helped Slocum pack all the stuff into the rig outside. They climbed aboard and

Slocum was just about to flick the reins to get the horse started, when Bouvier stopped him. "Hold on a minute," he said. Slocum saw that Bouvier was looking across the street toward the saloon. He looked, too, and he saw the four cowboys coming out. They moved to their horses, gathered their reins and started to climb into their saddles. Then all four cowboys went down as the saddles all slipped off the horses. The cowboys landed hard and sent up a big cloud of dust. As they cussed and yelled, getting up to their feet and dusting themselves off, Bouvier roared out laughing.

Slocum could sense trouble coming. He climbed down out of the rig, with the rig between himself and the cowboys across the street. One of the cowboys turned and looked at Bouvier sitting in the rig and laughing. In another instant, all four were lined up and staring at Bouvier. Slocum eased around to the back of the rig.

"You think that was funny?" a cowboy called across the street to Bouvier.

"It looked funny from over here," Bouvier answered.

"Them straps was cut," the cowboy said. "I don't s'pose you know nothing about that?"

"What would I know?" Bouvier said. "I been right over here since I come into town."

"I say you know," the cowboy said. "I say you done it yourself."

Bouvier shrugged. "Think what you want," he said.

"Let's go over there and stomp his ass," said another of the hands.

Slocum stepped out into clear view. "Four against two ain't such bad odds," he said. "Come on ahead, boys."

The four men had started moving toward Bouvier, but when Slocum appeared, they stopped. Then one of them said, "We can take them both. Come on."

"Hold up," Slocum said. "If you want to duke it out, let's all take off our guns."

"That's all right with me," said one of the Young cowboys.

"Wait a minute," said another. "Ain't that Slocum over there?"

"Is it?" said the first one. "Hey, mister. Is your name Slocum?"

"That's right," Slocum said.

"He's a professional killer," said the cowboy who had recognized him. "I ain't messing with him."

"Let it go," said another one.

The four hands turned and walked back to their horses. Each one bent down and picked up his saddle, and they all started walking toward the stable. Bouvier laughed out loud.

"Knock it off," Slocum said. "We just got out of a fight. Don't push it."

"Hell," said Bouvier, "I thought a fight was what we was looking for."

"Not like that," Slocum said. "You still got all your teeth?"

"Sure, I do," Bouvier said.

"You ought to try to keep it that way," said Slocum. "Let's get back to the ranch."

Slocum climbed back up onto the seat and picked up the reins. He started them up with a lurch and headed out of town. As they drove past the cowboys walking and carrying their saddles, Bouvier turned and gave them a wide grin. Slocum didn't see it. Rolling on out of town, Slocum asked Bouvier, "Did you cut their cinches?"

"No, I never," Bouvier said. "I seen it done though. I watched while a little kid done it, so I knowed they was going to take a tumble. I was waiting for it to happen."

"Why would a kid cut four cinch straps?" Slocum said.

"Damned if I know," said Bouvier. "Must be a mean little shit. He didn't even stick around to watch the fun."

They drove on a little farther, and then Bouvier said, "I give the kid a dollar and a jackknife to do it."

Slocum kept driving. "I figured as much," he said. After a few more minutes of silence, he added, "It was kind of funny."

That night Charley Bouvier went back to town. He took along with him another cowhand named Tod Billingsley.

They rode straight to the Red Ass Saloon, hitched their horses, and went inside. Bellied up to the bar, they ordered their drinks. Tod said low to Bouvier, "Hey, Charley, don't look now, but there's old man Young and some of his boys over there at a table."

Bouvier looked over his shoulder and saw Young, one of the cowboys who had been a victim of his earlier prank, and a third man he did not recognize. The stranger had a look different from that of any of Young's cowhands or even his hired toughs. He was a man probably in his thirties, with black hair and a black handlebar mustache. He was wearing the trousers and vest of a black suit with a white shirt, and a flat-brimmed black hat was pulled down low on his forehead. As Bouvier took note, the cowhand leaned toward Young and spoke low, and it seemed to Bouvier that he was being indicated.

"Yeah," Bouvier said to Tod. "I see them. They see me too. I think that one is telling ole Young over there that it was me that dumped him and his buddies into the street today." He chuckled at his recollection of the scene.

The bartender brought their drinks, and Tod Billingsley drank his down. "Let's get out of here, Charley," he said.

"I ain't skeered a that bunch," Bouvier said.

"Me neither," said Tod, "but there ain't no sense in us getting ourselves into a fight here. Come on, Charley. Let's go."

"That's the second time I've heard that said today," Bouvier said. "I'm getting kinda tired of it. Hell, they been killing our cows and our boys. How come we're s'posed to be so damn polite? If I want to have myself a drink in a public saloon, I'll have it. Ain't no one going to run me off."

"If Mr. Jimson was here," Tod said, "he'd tell us to clear out. Slocum would, too."

"You pretty sure of that, are you?" said Bouvier. He tossed down his own drink and turned to leave. "Shit," he said. "Come on."

As Bouvier and Tod walked through the swinging doors, the stranger at Parley Young's table stood up. He gave a hitch to his gun belt, then headed for the door. As he stepped out, Bouvier and Tod were just loosening the reins of their mounts from around the hitch rail.

"Howdy, boys," said the stranger.

The two cowboys looked up.

"You talking to us?" Bouvier asked the stranger.

"I don't see no one else out here," the stranger said.

"We were just leaving," Tod said.

"I can see that," the stranger said. "I heard that someone's been cutting cinch straps around town. Thought I'd check and make sure yours is all right."

Bouvier checked his. "It's all right," he said.

"Mine, too," said Tod.

"What kind of chicken shit would do that to a man's cinch strap?" the stranger asked.

"I—I don't know," Tod said.

"Maybe not," the stranger said, "but I bet your buddy here knows. That right, chicken shit?"

"Now look here, mister—"

"Parsons," said the stranger. "Aaron Parsons. You heard of me?"

"No," said Bouvier. "I don't—"

"One Shot," said Tod.

"That's what some calls me," Parsons said. "That's most usually all it takes me. One shot."

"Well, I think we better be getting along, Mr. Parsons," said Tod.

"Go right along," Parsons said. "Don't let me hold you up. But I don't know why you'd want to ride along with a cinch-strap-cutting chicken shit like that."

Bouvier had taken as much as he could stand. He straightened up and stepped out away from his horse, out into the street, and he held his gun hand out ready for action. He was nervous, and it showed, but he wasn't going to back out of this. He wasn't going to be called names either.

"You watch who you're calling names, mister," he said. "I don't even know you."

"I introduced myself, didn't I?" said Parsons. "And, hell,

I know your name already. It's chicken shit."

Bouvier went for his gun, but Aaron Parsons was much too fast for the cowboy. One Shot's gun was out and had blasted a hole in Bouvier's head before Bouvier had even had time to clear leather. Bouvier's head jerked with the impact, and he sank to his knees, then fell over on his face. He twitched once. He was dead. Parsons turned his gun on Tod, but Tod had his hands in the air.

"I ain't fighting you," Tod said.

"You just made a wise decision. Now you'd best load that chicken shit up and take him home," Parsons said. He holstered his six-gun, turned, and walked back into the Red Ass. With trembling hands, Tod loaded the body. Then he mounted up and, leading the horse with the grim load, headed out of town. There were tears in his eyes, and there was blood on his hands and on his shirtfront.

10

Buttermilk sensed that someone was coming up behind him on the trail. He didn't want to fall too far behind the stagecoach, but he did want to know who was riding up on his backside. He waited until he found a likely place on the trail where he could ride off to the side behind a clump of trees and hide and watch. Sure enough, it wasn't long before Snider came riding by. He wasn't in a hurry. Buttermilk recognized Snider right away as one of Young's crew. His first impulse was to move out and challenge the man, but he decided instead to reverse the situation. He let Snider go on by, and then he started riding in Snider's tracks, keeping an eye on Snider to see if the man meant to attack the coach all alone or what. He was surprised to find that Snider continued just riding along not in much of a rush. Buttermilk waited awhile, then moved out onto the trail again and let Snider set the pace.

When at long last they arrived in the capital, Buttermilk was pleased to see that the place was so busy. It would be easier for him to remain incognito. The town wasn't all that big, but it was full of people, and the streets were crowded with wagons, men riding horseback, all seeming to be in a hurry to get somewhere. Buttermilk was able to watch Carl

Jimson check into a hotel. Then he saw that Snider waited a bit, then checked into the same hotel. Buttermilk put his horse in a stable and then made his way back to the big hotel. Still trying to keep himself hidden in the bustling crowd, he watched Snider go into the saloon just off the hotel lobby and buy himself a drink. Jimson went into the dining room and ordered a meal. Buttermilk watched as Snider finished his drink, then moved to spy on Jimson. Only when Jimson had finished his meal and gone to his room for the night did Snider seem to relax and get serious about his drinking. At that point, Buttermilk went out to the main desk and got himself a room for the night. He decided to get himself a good night's sleep and be up early the next morning.

Tod Billingsley rode slowly up to the ranch house, leading the horse that bore the body of Charley Bouvier. Slocum was on the porch and saw them coming. He stood up and tossed aside the cigar he was smoking, stepped off the porch, and walked out to meet the long-faced cowboy. He could tell right away that the body on the other horse was that of Bouvier. "What happened?" he asked Tod.

"I couldn't stop him, Mr. Slocum," Tod said. "We was in the Red Ass. Charley let himself get crowded into a fight with a gunslinger. I tried to get him out of there, but he wouldn't listen to me. He was suckered all right. He never had a chance."

"One of Young's men?" Slocum asked.

"He was with Young," Tod said, "but I never seen him before. He's new. I tell you, Mr. Slocum, he was slick. And fast. A real cold-blooded killer, too. He deliberately egged Charley on to get him to draw on him. I couldn't do nothing about it. I was too skeered."

"So Young's brought himself in a hired gunhand," Slocum mused.

"He called himself Aaron something or other," Tod said. "One Shot."

"Aaron Parsons," Slocum said. "I know him. He's good, all right. One of the best. Damn. I wonder what Young is up to. Well, get some of the boys together. We'd best take care of Charley here."

Carl Jimson had finished up his breakfast of ham and eggs and was walking down the street toward the governor's office in the capitol. Buttermilk was lurking in the shadows between two buildings along the way. He thought that he had kept himself well hidden. He had moved out ahead of Jimson, knowing that Jimson would make a beeline for the capital, and he meant to keep his eyes on his boss to make sure that the old man ran into no trouble. He hadn't yet seen Snider that morning. As Jimson walked by the narrow passageway where Buttermilk was skulking, he said, "You might as well come on out of there, Buttermilk."

Buttermilk, humiliated, came out, but Jimson had not slowed his pace. Buttermilk hurried to catch up and walk alongside Jimson. "How'd you know I was in there?" Buttermilk said. "I thought I was pretty well hid."

"Hell, I've known you were following me since yesterday morning," Jimson said. "Whose bright idea was that anyhow?"

"Aw, Slocum told me I had ought to follow along," said Buttermilk, "just in case them men of Young's should try anything else. You know, after they had tried to stop the coach. You ain't mad about it, are you?"

"No," Jimson said. "I appreciate your concern. Slocum's, too. But I don't think they'll try anything here in the capital. There's too many lawmen here in this town."

"They might try again on your way back home though," Buttermilk said. "And besides that, one of them's here."

Jimson stopped walking and turned to look Buttermilk in the face.

"Here at the capital?" he said. "One of Young's men?"

"Yes sir," said Buttermilk. "That's right. He come along behind me out on the trail, and I fell back and got behind him. He ain't tried nothing yet. He's just been keeping an eye on you. Hell, I imagine he's watching us right now. It's that Snider is who it is."

"His assignment might just be to find out what I accomplish here," Jimson said. "If he had anything more in mind, he wouldn't likely be alone. Well, keep a sharp lookout just to make sure he don't try anything more than spying."

"Yes sir," Buttermilk said. Jimson started walking again at his previous brisk pace. In a few more minutes, the two men walked together into the big capital. Outside the governor's office, Jimson said to Buttermilk, "Wait here." Then, as Buttermilk took a chair, he moved on over to a receptionist sitting behind a desk. "Hello. I'm Carl Jimson," he said. "I'm here to see Governor Davis."

"Do you have an appointment?" the lady asked.

"No," Jimson said, "but my business is urgent, and if you'll just announce me, I'm sure the governor will see me."

"The governor is very busy today, Mr. Jenson," the receptionist said. "Let me make you an appointment for—"

"I rode a stagecoach for two days to get here," Jimson said. "I have some serious business to discuss with Bob, and my name is Jimson, not Jenson. Now if you don't go in there and tell him I'm out here, I'll just barge on in unannounced."

"Oh, you can't do that, sir," the lady said.

"You watch me," Jimson said, starting to walk around her desk. She jumped up, quickly moving between Jimson and the door.

"No. No," she said. "Wait."

She hurried through the door, closing it fast behind her, and in another minute, she reappeared with a sheepish look on her face. She held the door open and stepped aside. "Go right in, Mr. Jimson," she said. "Governor Davis will see you."

"Thank you," said Jimson, walking past her, and he muttered, "Damn right he'll see me."

Inside the office Governor Davis stood up with a wide grin on his face and walked around his big desk to meet Jimson. He held out a hand, which Jimson took. "Carl," the governor said warmly, "it's good to see you. What brings you to town?"

"I'll get right to business," Jimson said. "You're too busy

for chitchat, and so am I. I've got big troubles at home. There's a range war brewing between me and Parley Young. I've been trying to ignore him, but he's pushed it to the limit now. He's killed some of my cattle, and then he went to killing cowhands. I went to Merle about it, but Merle kept saying we had no proof. Now Merle's been killed. Now, Bob, I could take my boys over there to Parley's place and wipe him out, but I don't want to do it like that. I had to come and see you first."

"You say Merle's been killed?" the governor asked.

"That's right," said Jimson.

"And Parley Young did it," the governor said, "or had it done?"

"I couldn't prove that in a court of law, Bob," Jimson said. "The last time I saw Merle I went to him with a complaint against Young. He told me he was going out to have a talk with him. The next time I saw him, his body had been dumped on my ranch."

"I'm glad you came, Carl," said Davis. "Sit down there. Sit down." As Jimson sat, Davis walked back around his desk and took his own seat. He furrowed his brow in thought. "Merle's dead. Goddamn it, why didn't you come to me sooner?" he asked.

"I was trying to let Merle handle the situation," said Jimson.

"All right," said the governor. "All right. Well, what can I do now?"

"There's no law down there anymore," Jimson said.

"Merle didn't have any deputies?" the governor asked.

"No. None. Have you got a marshal you can send back down with me to take charge of the situation?"

"I haven't got anyone here I can spare," Davis said.

"Damn it, Bob," said Jimson. "We got to have something. What do you suggest? That I just go on ahead and engage in all-out war?"

"I don't have anyone I can send," Davis said, "but I think maybe there is something I can do for you." He pulled open a desk drawer and withdrew some paper. Then he reached for the pen on his desk. As he started writing, he asked

Jimson, "Do you have some reliable men you can count on to back you up if it comes to a fight?"

"I've got good men," Jimson said, "but they're young and they're cowhands. I have one gunfighter. He's with me because Young's men beat him up, and I let him stay at my place to heal. He's a good man and he's willing to help. In fact, he drove off an attack on the stagecoach right after I left home to come up here. Name's Slocum."

The governor stopped writing and looked up at Jimson. "John Slocum?" he asked.

"That's right," said Jimson. "You know him?"

"I know of him," said Davis. "He's got quite a reputation."

"Good or bad?" Jimson asked.

"It depends on who you're talking to," the governor said. "As far as I know, he's not wanted for anything here—or anywhere else that I'm aware of. But he's sure been into plenty of scraps."

"Well, he's been straight with me," Jimson said, "and he's been a help."

"That's good enough for me," said Davis. He laid aside his pen, took up a blotter, and blotted the ink. Then he handed the paper to Jimson.

"Me?" said Jimson. "A marshal?"

"That's right," Davis said. "With full authority. It'll only be until you get the mess down there cleaned up, and you can get a new sheriff elected. In the meantime, you can deputize all the help you need. The only thing is, there's no pay involved. I suggest you deputize all your hands and Slocum, too. It's up to you, Carl. Clean it up."

Buttermilk jumped to his feet as Jimson came back out of the office, tucking a folded paper into his inside coat pocket. "Thank you, ma'am," the newly appointed marshal said to the receptionist as he passed her by. "Let's go, Buttermilk," he said. "I think we can still catch the stage out today if we hurry."

"That sure didn't take you long," Buttermilk said. "Did you do any good in there, do you think?"

"Yes, I did," Jimson said. "I surely did."

"Is the governor sending a marshal back down with us?"

"Nope."

"Militia?"

"No."

"Well, what then?"

"Just you and me, Buttermilk," Jimson said. "Just you and me."

He stopped and pulled out the paper from his pocket, unfolded it, and showed it to Buttermilk. Buttermilk read it slowly and carefully. "I'll be damned," he said. "He made you a marshal. Did I read that right? He made you a marshal?"

"That's right," Jimson said. "It's temporary. Till we get this business settled. And, by the way, you're my first deputy."

"You can make me a deputy?"

"I just did," Jimson said. "Come on. Let's go. I want to make that stage. We've got a lot of work to do."

They walked on out of the building and started down the street, headed back for the hotel, and Buttermilk caught a glimpse of Snider standing across the street. "Mr. Jimson," he said, "there's that Snider over there."

"I see him," said Jimson. "Don't let on that we see him though."

"What do you want me to do?"

"Just act like we don't know he's there," Jimson said.

"When he starts in to follow that stage back," said Buttermilk, "I could stop him out on the trail real easy."

"No," Jimson said. "Don't do anything. Not unless he starts to do something first. Let him ride on back to Parley Young and tell Parley that I left the governor's office empty-handed and alone. Let Parley get all puffed up thinking that I failed in my mission. We'll have him off guard that way."

"Well, all right," Buttermilk said. "You're the boss. But if it was up to me, I'd take him out somewhere along the trail. It'd be one less of them no-good bastards to have to deal with later on."

"Do it my way, Buttermilk," Jimson said. "We'll get them all, and it'll all be according to the law."

Since Snider had already seen Buttermilk, Jimson decided that Buttermilk might just as well ride back with him on the stage, his horse tied to the back. He wasn't looking forward to the long trip back home alone. They got their stuff together and made the stage in plenty of time. Soon they were back on the road. Buttermilk sat facing the rear, and he watched out the windows as they moved along. He and Jimson were the only two passengers. They had gone but a few miles out of the capital when Buttermilk saw what he was watching for.

"Snider's out there," he said. "Looks like he's trying to stay out of sight."

"Stay alert," Jimson said.

"He's disappeared over the rise," said Buttermilk. "Mr. Jimson, I'd feel a whole lot better if I was to get out and keep a good watch on him."

Jimson sighed a heavy sigh. "All right," he said. "Suit yourself."

The stage slowed for a sharp curve in the road, and Buttermilk opened the door and jumped out. As the stage rolled on past him, he caught up to his horse and loosened the reins. Then he mounted up and rode off to the side of the road cautiously. He searched out a piece of high ground and made his way to the top. Then he spotted Snider. Snider had not noticed him, it seemed. Buttermilk dogged Snider's trail for another couple of miles until it became obvious that Snider's intention was to pass the stage by. Then Buttermilk rode back to the stage. He tied his horse on behind again and climbed back into the coach.

"He's gone on ahead," he said.

"Like I figured," said Jimson. "He's going straight to Young to report on what he saw at the capital. I think we can go on and relax till we get back to the ranch, at least till we get back to Harleyville."

"You go on ahead and do just that, Mr. Jimson," Buttermilk said. "I think I'll just keep my eyes open. Just in case."

•   •   •

On the porch of the Jimson ranch house, Felicia came out to sit with Slocum, who was smoking a cigar and sipping coffee. He stood up to greet her. Then they both sat down.

"You're feeling a lot better, aren't you?" she asked him.

"Does it show?" he said.

She smiled. "Yeah," she said. "It does."

"Well," he said, "you're right. I feel most good as new."

"What are you going to do about poor Charley?" she asked him.

"I'm not going to do anything," he said. "Just try to keep everyone here alert. That's all. I'm not the boss here, and ole Jimson seems to want us to sit tight and not go raiding onto Young's place or starting any fights. So we just sit here and keep our eyes open. I'll try to keep any more of the boys from going into town though, at least till the boss gets back."

"It just makes me sick," Felicia said. "All the killing. It could be anyone next. It could be you—or Buttermilk."

"Don't go worrying about me," Slocum said. "I've been through plenty of fights. I've been banged up some, but I've always mended. And Buttermilk can handle himself pretty well, too. I've seen him in action."

He wondered if it would comfort her any to know that Buttermilk was in actuality the notorious Rock Port Kid. He knew that he'd have to leave it to Buttermilk to tell her, though, if he wanted her to know.

"It's him you're really worried about, isn't it?" he asked her.

"Yeah," she admitted. "It really is. I'm sorry, John, after what we—"

"Hey," he said, interrupting her. "Don't you worry your head about that either. Ole Buttermilk's a fine young man. You could do a whole lot worse than get your clutches into him. I'm all for it, and anything I can do to help, you just let me know. Why, hell, I'll rope him and brand him for you if you want."

Felicia laughed at that, and Slocum was glad. She'd had a rough time, and for everyone at the Jimson ranch, there'd been too much sorrow, too much worry, too many frowns. It was good to see someone laugh for a change, and he was glad that it was Felicia. She caught up her laughter.

"I don't think you'll have to do that," she said. "But if I find out I'm wrong, and I can't catch him by myself, I might just take you up on that offer. Slocum?"

"What?"

"Does Buttermilk know that you and me—was together that one night?"

"He never heard it from me," Slocum said, "and he won't either."

"Thanks," she said. "But he does know what I was."

"From what I've seen," said Slocum, "he's not bothered by that. So don't you be. Just think about what happens from right now on. Don't let the past get in your way. Yours or his."

She gave Slocum a puzzled look and leaned forward.

"What about his?" she said.

"Huh?"

"What about Buttermilk's past?" she asked.

"Oh, nothing," said Slocum. "You just never know about a man's past. Even a young man like that. Why, you don't know how many gals he's been with, do you?"

"No," she said. " 'Course I don't."

"Does it bother you?"

"No.

"There," he said. "That's all I meant."

11

Buttermilk was on horseback again. They were getting close to Harleyville, and he felt the need to do some more checking. Topping a rise, he saw Snider not far ahead. Jimson had told him to let Snider alone, that he would take care of things according to the law. But Buttermilk had his own feelings about the situation, and Jimson was not there to watch. He rode hard and came up behind Snider in short order. When Snider heard the hooves pounding behind him, he turned in the saddle, and he was startled to see that Buttermilk already had him covered with a six-gun.

"What the hell?" he said, raising his hands. "What is this?"

"You been dogging Mr. Jimson's trail," Buttermilk said.

"I didn't do nothing," said Snider. "I was on business. That's all."

"Yeah," Buttermilk said. "Your business was spying on Mr. Jimson. I watched you the whole time. Drop your guns. Real easy."

Snider eased the six-gun out of his holster and let it drop.

"Now the rifle," said Buttermilk.

Snider withdrew the rifle from the scabbard and dropped it to the ground.

"Ride ahead a bit," Buttermilk ordered, and as Snider moved forward, so did Buttermilk. Then he told Snider to dismount. Buttermilk got off his horse and picked up Snider's weapons. Then he climbed back into the saddle. He rode on up to where Snider was standing beside his horse. Then he took hold of the horse's reins and started to ride off, leading Snider's mount. "Have a nice walk on into Harleyville," he said.

"Hey," Snider shouted. "Hey, you can't do that to me. Goddamn you."

Young, Orwig, Parsons, and two other toughs sat together in the Red Ass waiting for the return of Snider. It was almost time for the stage to arrive, and Young had told Snider to get back ahead of it. He was getting impatient. So were the rest of his gang, with the exception of Parsons. He sat calmly drinking coffee. The others drank whiskey.

"Where's that damned Snider?" Young said.

"He ought to be back by now, Boss," said Orwig.

"That stage will be here just anytime now," Young said. "Damn it. I need to know what Jimson was able to get done over there."

"What's the difference?" Parsons said.

"He might be bringing lawmen back with him," Young said. "That's the difference. There's no telling what he might have talked the goddamned governor into. He could be bringing back a posse or something."

"Have they got any charges filed on you?" Parsons asked.

"No," Young said. " 'Course not. I've been too careful for that."

"Then what's your worry?" said Parsons. "A lawman, twenty lawmen, can't do a damn thing to you if there ain't no charges filed."

"Well, I guess you're right about that," Young said, "but even so, me and Jimson are at war, and he's got the governor on his side. I need to know what the hell his next move will be."

"Let's just ask him when he gets here," Parsons said.

"What?" said Young. "Ask him?"

• • •

Slocum rode toward Harleyville to meet the stage with Jimson on it. He figured that Buttermilk would be watching it, all right, but he wanted to make sure that there would be no problems with the Young gang on Jimson's return. There was no telling what that bunch might try to pull. He rode easy, knowing that he had plenty of time before the stagecoach's arrival. Riding along, he had time to think, and he wondered just what Jimson's trip might have accomplished. Would the governor actually send some help in the form of lawmen? Slocum was not anxious to have lawmen arrive, but then, he thought, if there were enough of them to take care of the situation, he could just ride on with a clear conscience. He no longer felt the need for personal vengeance. That had been satisfied.

The stage rolled into Harleyville early, a rare occurrence. One of Young's men was watching at the front window of the Red Ass. "Here it comes," he said. "There's two horses tied on behind."

"Let's go," said Parsons. He stood up and led the way to the door and on outside. Buttermilk was just coming out the door of the stage when he found himself looking down the long barrel of Parsons's already cocked revolver. On the other side of the stage, Jimson found himself facing two armed toughs. Young stepped out of the Red Ass, and the driver and a shotgun gave him a look.

"Just go on about your business," Young said to them. "This don't concern you."

Parsons had Jimson and Buttermilk standing side by side by then, and the others took their guns. Young stepped out into the street. Looking at the two horses behind the stage, he recognized the one Snider had been riding.

"You got my horse there," he said. "Where'd you get it?"

"Found it outside of town," Buttermilk said.

"What happened to the rider?" Young asked.

"He'll be along," said Buttermilk. "He's walking, so it'll take him a spell."

"What do you want to do with this one?" Parsons asked Young, indicating Buttermilk.

"We don't need him," Young said.

"You like setting people afoot," Parsons said. "Get to walking."

Buttermilk hesitated, but Jimson said, "Go on, Buttermilk. Do what he says."

Buttermilk started walking out of town in the direction of the Jimson spread. Young looked at Jimson and said, "Get on his horse. We're going for a little ride."

"That's kidnapping," Jimson said.

"Mount up," said Parsons, and his voice was cold and his eyes were steely. Jimson took note and moved to Buttermilk's horse. He climbed up into the saddle. Young's gun hands brought all their horses, and the whole bunch swung into their saddles.

"Let's go," Young said, and taking Jimson with them, they headed out, riding toward the Young ranch.

Buttermilk had not walked far when Slocum met him on the road. "What's happened?" Slocum asked him, and Buttermilk related the episode in town.

"Damn," Slocum said. "I meant to be there when the stage came in."

"Son of a bitch was early for once," Buttermilk said. "Of all times."

"Well, get on, and let's go," Slocum said, giving Buttermilk an arm. Buttermilk swung up on the big Appaloosa behind Slocum, and Slocum urged the horse into a run toward town. At the stage depot, the driver gave Buttermilk his six-gun.

"They throwed it in the street after you walked on," he said.

"Thanks," said Buttermilk, holstering the gun. "What did they do with Mr. Jimson?"

"They all rode out of town," the driver said. "Took him with them."

"Which way?" Slocum asked.

"Out toward Young's place," the man said.

"Go on," said Buttermilk. "I'll grab me a horse and follow you."

Slocum turned and rode hard again, this time on Young's trail. He had some ideas what Young and his bunch might do to Jimson, and he didn't like any of them. He hoped that he could catch them in time to prevent any of them from taking place. Since they were headed for the Young ranch, he figured they wouldn't do anything until they got there. He wanted to catch up to them before then if possible. It didn't happen though. At the gate onto the Young property, he could see them dismounted at the ranch headquarters. He stopped the Appaloosa. It wouldn't do anyone any good to go charging the house. He could tell it was well guarded. He sat there in his saddle, studying the situation for a couple of minutes, and then Buttermilk rode up beside him.

"I couldn't catch them in time," Slocum said. "They took him in the house."

"What the hell are they up to?" Buttermilk asked.

"Only one thing I can think of," Slocum said. "They're going to try to make him sign over his ranch. If they can make him do it, then they'll kill him. They can't leave him alive to take them to court and tell that they forced him into it."

"What'll we do?" Buttermilk asked.

"You go on back to the ranch and get most of the boys," Slocum said. "Just leave a couple of them back there to look out for the women. Just in case. I'll try to keep them busy enough in there that they don't do anything to Jimson till you get back."

"Okay," Buttermilk said. He turned his horse and headed for the Jimson ranch as fast as he could go. Slocum watched him go for a minute, then looked back toward the Young headquarters ahead. He would have to think of something, and fast.

Inside the Young house, Jimson gestured toward the chair behind his big desk. "Have a seat, Carl," he said.

"Damn it," said Jimson, "what's this all about?"

"I just want to strike a deal with you," said Young. "That's all. That was the only way I could think of to get you to sit down and talk sense with me. Now, I've made you a good offer on your place already. I'm a fair man. It still stands. I'll pay you in cash, right now, if you'll just write up the papers and sign them."

"Then what?" Jimson asked.

"Why, then, I'll give you a reasonable period of time to pack up and move out," said Young. "Like I said, I'm a fair man. What do you say?"

"I've told you before, Parley," said Jimson, "that my place is not for sale. It's still not for sale. Not to you. Not for any price."

Parsons stepped up beside Young and looked hard at Jimson. He smacked his right fist into his left palm.

"Listen to reason, Carl," said Young. "I want your place, and I mean to get it. I'm trying to be fair with you, but I'm about out of being patient."

"If I was to sign that paper you want," Jimson said, "I doubt I'd live to go home and pack. All I'd have to do would be to take you to court and tell how you kidnapped me and forced me to sign. No court would hold me to that signature, and you know it. That's why you mean to kill me."

"I don't have any such intention," Young said. "I'm just trying to reason with you here. That's all. Now I know that you just got back from visiting with your friend the governor, and I know that it didn't do you no good. You come on back home all by your lonesome. You thought you were going to get some lawmen sent down here to help you fight me off, but you didn't get any. Even if you had got them, you got no proof of any wrongdoing on my part. That's because I ain't broke no laws. You got me all wrong. I'm just an honest businessman trying to make an honest deal here."

Jimson reached in to the inside pocket of his jacket and pulled out the paper from the governor's office. He tossed it on the desk.

"Read that," he said. "And I do have something illegal

on you that I can make stick in any court of law. I charge you with kidnapping, and I'm placing you under arrest, right now."

Young picked up the paper, unfolded it, and read it carefully. He read it again, as if he couldn't believe it the first time through. He handed it to Parsons without a word. Parsons read it and tossed it back down on the desk.

"Sign them other papers," he said, "and you can get on with your new job."

"Just who the hell are you?" Jimson asked.

"Name's Aaron Parsons," the gunfighter said. "You heard of me?"

"They call him One Shot," said Young. "I'm sorry I forgot to introduce you sooner. Are you going to sign your ranch over, or not?"

"Hell no," Jimson said.

"Well, I'm shit out of patience," said Young. He looked at Parsons. "You take over," he said, and he turned and walked out of the house to his front porch. Parsons stepped toward Jimson.

"I ain't nice like Mr. Young," he said. "I ain't fixing to reason with you. I mean to break every bone in your body except for your right hand till you sign that paper."

"And you'll kill me after I sign it, and Parley Young will never pay my widow a dime," Jimson said. "Go on. Do your worst."

"Mr. Young never said I was to kill you," Parsons said. "Just get you to sign."

Suddenly Parsons smacked Jimson across the side of the face with the back of his hand.

"All right, all right," Jimson said. "At least once I sign you'll kill me quick and get it over with."

As Jimson looked at the paper on the desk that Young had prepared, Parsons grinned an evil grin. "Shit," he said. "That was almost too damn easy." Jimson took up the pen on the desk and dipped it in the inkwell. On the bottom of the page, he wrote, "Karl Jemsen."

"There," he said. "It's done. Kill me or let me go."

Parsons took the paper and looked at it. He carried it to

the front door, opened the door, and called out, "I've got it." Young appeared at the door and looked at the paper. He smiled a broad smile and stepped back inside.

"Well, well," he said, "that's more like it. I'm glad you finally came to your senses. Now I guess I'll have to pay you."

"You really mean to pay me?" Jimson said.

"Sure I do," said Young. "I said I would. Pay the man for me, One Shot."

Young started back for the front door just as a bullet smashed through the front window of his house. He dropped down to the floor. Parsons pulled his six-gun and ran to a window to look out.

"I can't see anyone out there," he said.

"Well, someone's sure as hell out there," said Young.

"That was a rifle shot," said Parsons. "I can't do no good with this six-gun, even if I spot him."

"There's rifles over there in the cabinet," said Young. "Go get one."

Parsons looked over his shoulder and spied the gun cabinet on the far wall. He holstered his six-gun and started toward the cabinet, but another shot rang out. Another window was smashed, and he dropped to his hands and knees. "Shit," he said, and he crawled toward the cabinet. Jimson jumped up from the chair and ran toward the cabinet. Grabbing all the rifles, he ran for the back door of the house.

"Stop him," Young shouted.

Parsons stood up to run after Jimson, but another bullet crashed through a window, and he fell to the floor again. Jimson made it out the back door, but just as he did, he saw the hands from the bunkhouse coming out in response to the shots. He turned to run around to the other side of the house. As he rounded the corner, a few shots from the Young hands followed him.

From his position near the front gate of the Young spread, Slocum saw Jimson come from behind the house. He also saw the ranch hands come out of the bunkhouse, and he saw them shoot at the old man. Jimson was in a tough spot.

As the ranch hands moved toward the house, Slocum fired a shot in their direction. It slowed them down. Some ran for cover. Jimson was to the right side of the house, and the gunnies were to its left. If Jimson tried to make a run for Slocum's position, someone inside the house or any one of those on the other side of the house would have clear shots at him. Slocum knew he could hold them off for a while, but he was one man with a rifle. And he had no way of giving Jimson a clear path out of there.

With some pleasure, he took note of the fact that none of the hands who had come running from the bunkhouse had taken the time to get a rifle, and he had seen the armload of rifles Jimson was carrying. He figured that it was all six-guns down there against his rifle. The distance was all in Slocum's favor, but it was no help at all to Jimson. As he watched, one of the ranch hands made a move to get closer to the house. Slocum snapped off a shot that kicked up dust at the man's feet. The man turned and ran back to his original position.

It took a little while, but Carl Jimson figured out the situation. He had one man out there in front with a rifle, holding all of Young's gang at bay. It would be a long run up to where his man was, and any one of the Young men would get a clear shot at him if he tried it. But the Young hands, except for Parsons inside the house, were all on the other side of the house from him. He decided that, instead of making for the man at the gate with the rifle, he could make a straight walk out from the side of the house. That way, neither the ones in the house nor the ones on the other side would be able to see him. He could move out that way until he was out of the range of their revolvers. Then he could start to make his way out to the road, where his man was waiting. Still carrying all the rifles from Young's cabinet, he started walking.

Slocum saw what Jimson was doing. It was a smart move. Now his own part would be to make sure that none of the Young crowd picked up on it, or if they did, to keep them back around the house with his rifle shots. He saw a man peeking from around the corner of the house, and he fired a shot at him. It smashed into the wall near the man's head, and the man disappeared back around the corner. Then just for good measure, Slocum sent another shot through one of the front windows.

12

Slocum heard the pounding hooves on the road behind him. He hoped it would be Buttermilk and a crew of Jimson's cowhands. He glanced over his shoulder, but he couldn't yet see them. He looked back toward the ranch house just in time to see a gunman step out into the open and take a bead on the fleeing Jimson. Quickly, he raised his rifle to his shoulder, took aim, and fired. The man jerked, twitched, and pitched forward to lie still. Jimson kept running. Slocum looked back again, and he could see the riders coming. In another minute he would be able to tell whether they were friendly or not. Shots came his way from the house, but they were six-gun shots and the range was too much for them.

He could see that Jimson had stopped running. He seemed to be on his knees, panting, trying to catch his breath, Slocum figured. He was out of the range of the six-guns though. He should be all right. Slocum kept his eyes on the house in case anyone should try to pursue Jimson or take any more pot shots at him. He shot another quick look over his shoulder and recognized Buttermilk riding at the head of the crew that was coming. Good.

In another minute or two Buttermilk and the other cowboys were right with Slocum. He told them to dismount and take up positions around him with their rifles. "No one down there's got a rifle," he said. "Right now, we got the advantage over them. Just keep anyone from taking shots at your boss down there."

"What's happened?" Buttermilk asked.

"I'll tell you later," Slocum said. "I'm going out there to join Jimson and make sure he gets back up here safe with us. Keep us covered."

"You got it," Buttermilk said.

As Slocum started toward Jimson, Buttermilk and the others fired a barrage at the ranch house. No shots were returned. Slocum hurried toward Jimson, who was still on his knees. He still held the armload of rifles from the house. Watching the house, Slocum ran up in front of Jimson.

"You all right?" he said.

"Yeah," Jimson said. He was still panting. "I ain't had a run like that in years though."

"Here," Slocum said, "let me have those rifles." He took them one at a time and broke them against the ground. "They won't get any more use out of these," he said. "Are you ready to move out again? We won't have to run. We're out of their range here, and we can keep it that way till we get back to the road. Buttermilk and the boys are up there now."

"Yeah," said Jimson. "I can make it."

Slocum gave him a hand up, and the two of them started the long walk back to the road.

Still panting some, Jimson told Slocum, "Sons of bitches kidnapped me. We got a charge on them now. They tried to force me to sign my ranch over to Parley. I signed, but I spelt my name wrong. They never noticed."

"Good for you," Slocum said.

"Anyhow," Jimson continued, "the governor give me a marshal's commission. I'm deputizing you and all my hands. We're the law here now, and I just arrested Young and that gunfighter of his."

"It doesn't seem to have done much good so far," Slocum said.

"They're stubborn," the old man said, "and mean."

They reached the road some distance to the right of Buttermilk and the rest, and turned to walk on over to join them.

"You done good, Slocum," Jimson said. "You saved my ass."

"It was Buttermilk," Slocum said. "I'd have done good if I'd been there to meet that stage."

"The damn thing was early," Jimson said. "First time in history."

They walked up to Buttermilk and the others. Buttermilk almost threw his arms around Jimson. "Damn," he said, "I'm glad to see you. I was sure worried. I ought to be shot for letting them grab you like that."

"It wasn't your fault," Jimson said. "What counts is that I got out, and you're here now. Boys, in case you all ain't heard the news, I'm marshal now, and you're all deputies. That bunch down there are all under arrest."

A few cheers went up, and when everyone was quiet again, Buttermilk said, "Well, what do we do now?"

"I'm going to try to talk them out of there," Jimson said. "Someone wave a white flag."

In the ranch house, watching through a broken front window, Aaron Parsons saw the white flag tied to a rifle barrel being waved back and forth. "They want a parley, Young," he said. "What do you say?"

Young looked up from where he was cowering on the floor. "Let's find out what they want to say," he said. Slowly he stood up and walked toward the door. He stopped and looked at Parsons. Parsons shrugged and reached for the door handle. He jerked the door open and waited, as if he expected someone to shoot. It was quiet. He stepped out onto the porch, and Young followed him. Knowing that his own men were hidden around the house, Young called out, "Hold your fire, boys. They want to talk."

Up at the road, Jimson walked forward. Buttermilk walked to his right, Slocum to his left. Young and Parsons stepped down off the porch and moved closer to the others. Almost close enough to each other for a six-gun shot, both parties stopped. "What do you want, Jimson?" Young called out.

"I'm trying to avoid a bunch of killings here," Jimson said. "You know I'm marshal. I showed you the commission. And you know that deed transfer I signed is worthless. Throw down your weapons and tell all your men to do the same. Ride into town with me to the jailhouse. You'll get a fair trial."

"That's what you wanted to say?" Parsons snarled.

"That's my offer," said Jimson. "Take it or leave it."

"I ain't going to no jail," Parsons said.

"If I don't like your offer," Young said, "what then?"

"We'll stay and fight it out with you," Jimson said, "to the end. We've got plenty of men and plenty of rifles. Don't be a damn fool."

Young hesitated a moment. Then he said, "We need to go talk it over with the others."

"Don't be too long about it," Jimson said.

Young and Parsons turned their backs on Jimson and walked back toward the house. Jimson let them go a few paces before turning toward the road. He and Slocum and Buttermilk went to rejoin their crew.

Near the porch of his house, Young called out, "Boys, come on in the house. They won't shoot. Come on in. We got to talk."

One by one, the gang outside showed themselves cautiously, then walked toward the porch and the front door. They crowded inside. Young waited until they were all in and the door was closed.

"Here's the situation," he said. "They got rifles and we don't. Now, I know some of you boys has got rifles back in the bunkhouse. We need to get to them so we can even up this here fight. Jimson and his boys think we're discussing whether we should give up or not, so here's my plan. I want you boys to walk out of here real casual like and stroll on over there and get your rifles. Then come back out ashooting. You'll take them by surprise that way. Take up positions out front. Try to get Jimson and Slocum first. You do that, and the others will all cave in."

The gang left the house to do Young's bidding, and Young looked at Parsons. "We've got to get out of here," he said. "We can go out the back way and get a couple of horses and be on our way before anyone knows the difference."

"You son of a bitch," Parsons said. "You're throwing your own boys to the wolves."

"Better them than us, ain't it?" Young said. "You go first and get the horses ready. I'll get all the cash out of my safe."

Parsons went out the back door while Young knelt at his safe. He opened it up and began stuffing his pockets with stacks of bills. The safe emptied, he followed Parsons out the back way. He knew that Jimson had him beat. It was too late to come up with another plan. Since Jimson had gotten to the governor and had managed to get himself commissioned marshal, Young knew that he no longer had any options. He simply had to get out with as much as he could and get away to some place of safety where he could start over. He wished that he didn't have to take Parsons along, but he'd had no choice there either. The man was right beside him, and the man was deadly.

Outside, he found Parsons waiting with two horses. Young climbed onto one, turned it, and kicked its sides. They started riding. "Where you headed?" Parsons asked.

"Into Harleyville," said Young. "It's safe as long as Jimson and his bunch are out here. I've got more money in the bank, and I want to make a withdrawal before we leave these parts."

"That sounds reasonable to me," Parsons said.

"They're taking too long," Slocum said. "I don't like it."

"We'll give them another couple of minutes," said Jimson. "I don't want any more killing if we can avoid it."

Just then the bunkhouse door flew open and men with rifles came running out, some shooting as they ran.

"Drop down," Slocum shouted. "Take cover."

"Damn it," Jimson said.

"They've got rifles now," said Buttermilk.

"Hey, Boss," called a cowboy down the line, "Jimmy's been hit."

"How bad?" Jimson asked.

"Smashed his arm," said the cowboy.

"Buttermilk," Jimson said, "take Jimmy into the doc. Get him patched up, and then take him to the house. Once you're there, you settle in for a good night's sleep. You been going too long already. In the morning, come back out here with a wagon. Bring all the supplies we need for a long spell. No telling how long we'll have to camp out here before we can smoke that bunch out. You got that?"

"Hell, Mr. Jimson," Buttermilk said, "I don't need no rest. I—"

"Just do as I said," Jimson snapped. "Go on now."

Jimmy's arm had already been wrapped with a bandanna by the time Buttermilk got to him. Keeping low, Buttermilk helped Jimmy back to the horses. They mounted up and rode away from the fight. Jimson glanced at Slocum.

"They'll run out of bullets before we will," he said. "We got them pinned down, but we can send out for supplies whenever we need them."

"I guess you're right," Slocum said.

"What would you do?" Jimson asked him.

"I don't know," said Slocum. "I guess you're right."

In Harleyville, Buttermilk helped Jimmy dismount and took him into the doctor's office. Jimmy winced as the doctor unwrapped the wound to look at it. "How bad is it, Doc?" Buttermilk asked.

The doctor studied for a bit before going to work. "It'll heal," he said.

Across the street, Young and Parsons got off their horses in front of the bank. They walked in together, Parsons pulling the saddlebags off his horse as he went. At the counter, a teller greeted Parley Young with a smile. "What can I do for you today?" he asked.

"I want to withdraw my money," Young said.

"How much, Mr. Young?" the teller asked.

"All of it," said Young. "Every penny."

The teller looked astonished.

"You heard me right," Young said.

It took a few minutes, but soon Young was stuffing more cash into his pockets.

"I want to make a withdrawal, too," said Parsons.

The teller looked even more puzzled.

"Do you have an account?" he asked.

Parsons pulled out his six-gun, cocked it, and pointed it at the clerk's face. A woman at the next window screamed.

"Shut up, lady," said Parsons. "Everyone just stay calm and no one will get hurt." He looked back at the teller and tossed his saddlebags onto the counter. "Start filling them up," he said, "and be quick about it."

The frightened teller did as he was told while Parsons shot glances around the bank to keep his eyes on everyone.

"Are you crazy?" Young said.

"What's crazy?" said Parsons. "We're already under arrest, ain't we? And we're skipping the country, ain't we?"

"Well, yes," said Young, "but—"

"Then shut up and pull your shooter and help me watch everyone," Parsons said. The clerk stuffed another handful of bills into the bag, and Parsons grabbed it. "That's enough," he said. "Let's get out of here." Then out loud to everyone in the bank, he added, "Anyone even looks out that door till we're out of town gets his head blowed off."

They went outside, mounted up, and rode out easy for a ways, then spurred their horses and hurried on away from town. Inside the bank no one said a word. They stood still, frightened by Parsons's threat.

Across the street, Buttermilk and Jimmy came out of the doctor's office, mounted their horses, and headed for the Jimson ranch. They had no idea what had taken place while they waited for the doctor to do his work on Jimmy's arm. They were out of town before a customer got bold enough to run out of the bank shouting, "Holdup! Holdup!"

At the ranch, Buttermilk saw Jimmy settled in the bunk-house. Then he went on over to the main house to see Molly. He knew that she would be worried. When he knocked on the door, Felicia opened it.

"Buttermilk," she said, and she threw her arms around him. "Oh, we've been so worried. But where's Mr. Jimson?"

Molly came hustling out of the kitchen, wiping her hands on a towel. Her face wore a worried look.

"What's happened?" she said.

"Mr. Jimson's all right," Buttermilk said, "but it has been one interesting day." He went on to tell the two women what had happened in Harleyville and how Jimson had managed to escape from Young. He told them about the seige that Jimson and the others had laid out at the Young place. And he told them about the marshal's commission that the governor had given to Jimson. "He told me to come on back here and get a night's sleep," he continued, "and to bring a supply wagon over there to them in the morning, but I ain't so sure about that. I think I'd ought to go on ahead and get the wagon loaded up and get back over there."

"Now, Buttermilk," Molly said, "you do just what Mr. Jimson told you to do. He knows best."

Buttermilk shuffled his feet and looked down at the floor. "Well, all right, ma'am," he said, "but I reckon it would be all right if I was to at least start getting the wagon loaded up tonight. That way I'll be able to roll out earlier in the morning."

"That would be all right," said Molly. "Load up what you can. I'll be up early and put some food together for you to pack in. While I'm doing that, you can hitch up the horses."

"Yes, ma'am," said Buttermilk. "I'll go on and pack some blankets and a bunch of rifles and ammunition. Whatever else I can think of that we can let set out all night. Then I'll turn in."

"Felicia," Molly said, "help me think of anything they might need, and let's start getting it together."

"Oh," Buttermilk said, "Jimmy was shot over there a while ago. I took him by the doc's in town and got him patched up. He's going to pull through okay, Doc said. But just in case anyone else gets hurt over there, we'd ought to have some bandages and stuff."

"We'll see to it," Molly said.

With the sun low in the sky, Slocum looked at Jimson. "We just going to sit this out all night?" he asked.

"That's my intention," said Jimson. "If we try to move in on them, especially after dark, someone's liable to get hurt. We'll have a couple of men stay awake and watch. We'll rotate them so no one has to stay awake too long."

"All right," Slocum said.

"How about you and me taking the first watch?" Jimson asked.

"That's fine with me," said Slocum. Jimson told the rest to turn in for the night, and the two men sat up watching the house in front of them for any sign of movement.

Some miles away, Parley Young, riding along beside Aaron Parsons, said, "It's getting late. Shouldn't we be looking for a place to camp for the night?"

"You dumb shit," said Parsons, "we didn't pack for no camping trip. We want to eat or have a drink of water even, we got to ride straight through to the next town."

13

Buttermilk was loading the wagon over near the corral when Felicia brought an armload of supplies in from the house. When he saw her, he almost dropped what he was doing and rushed to her aid.

"Here," he said, "let me take that."

"I'm all right," she said, but he took the load away from her anyway. Then he stashed it in the wagon and redistributed it some.

"You're a careful packer," she said.

"I don't want to lose anything on the way over," he said. "Nor bang anything around any more than I have to."

"Is it going to be dangerous over there in the morning?" she asked him.

"It will be for the other side," he said. "Why, with me and Slocum both on our side, we can't lose. And now that we represent the law, shucks, I don't see what could go wrong."

"I sure hope you're right," she said. "I wouldn't want anything bad to happen to you—any of you."

"Thanks, Felicia," he said. "Well, I guess that's about all I can do till morning. Unless Miz Jimson has anything more to send out from the house."

"She hasn't," Felicia said. "She told me that was all of it till morning. She told me I could go on to bed."

"Oh," Buttermilk said. "I guess you've had a long day all right."

"I'm not tired," she said. "How about you?"

"Me?" he said. "Shoot. I'm going strong."

"You want to walk?" she asked him.

"Yeah," he said. "I'd like that fine."

She took his hand, and the touch of her sent thrills through his body. They began to stroll away from the wagon, away from the house, out into the darkness. They walked along for a few moments in silence. Buttermilk stopped, took Felicia by the shoulders, and turned her to face him.

"Felicia," he said, "there's something—"

She pulled his face down to hers and interrupted him with a kiss full on his lips. He thought that he would burst. At last she released him. He caught his breath.

"Felicia," he said, "I—I like you—a lot."

"I like you, too," she said.

"I mean, well, I mean more than that," he said. "But there's something I got to tell you about before I let this go on."

"It doesn't matter," she said. "Let it go on. And on and on."

"No," he said. "Listen to me. Please."

"All right," she said. "What is it."

"Buttermilk Smith ain't my real name," he said.

"I didn't think your mother named you Buttermilk," she said.

"Yeah, well, I wasn't born no Smith neither," he said. "My real name ain't too important, but what might be is that I was known as the Rock Port Kid. I got to be pretty famous, I guess, and the reason was that I done a bunch of killings. I never done no murders, but I got in a lot of fights in a range war down Texas way. There was a whole mess of men after me, and I just got to where I didn't want to live that kind of life no more. I changed my name and come up here, and Mr. Jimson give me a new start. Well, that's it. I just thought that you should ought to know about it. That's all."

"Thanks for telling me," she said. "But it doesn't make any difference in the way I feel about you. Well, it does, too. It just makes me like you more 'cause you told me."

"You mean that?" he said.

"Sure I do," she said. "But then, since you started this, there's something I want to ask you."

"Okay," he said. "Just ask. Ask me anything you want to."

"You know what I was before I came out here to the ranch," she said, and it wasn't really a question. Buttermilk was glad that it had gotten dark, because he felt his face flush.

"I know," he said.

"And it doesn't bother you at all?" she asked.

"Nothing that happened before tonight makes any difference to me," he said. "Felicia, I love you, and I want us to get hitched. I mean, I want to marry you. Will you? Will you have me?"

"Oh yes," she said, and she threw her arms around him and squeezed him tight. Then she kissed him again. He thought his head would explode. At last she moved back to his side and took his hand again and resumed their stroll. She headed back toward the wagon. Buttermilk figured that she would be saying good night to him soon. He hated the thought of parting company with her, but he knew that it made good sense. They would be up early in the morning.

When they reached the wagon, where their stroll had begun, she didn't stop, and she didn't turn toward the house. She strolled past the wagon and on toward the barn. Buttermilk didn't say anything. He let her lead the way. Soon they were inside the big, dark barn and over beside a large haystack. She pulled his face to her and kissed him again. Buttermilk wanted to be a gentleman, but he could only take so much of the closeness of her sweet flesh. He felt the bulge in his crotch. She pressed against him, and he knew that she could feel it, too.

"Felicia," he said.

"We're going to be married," she said. "We love each other. We don't have to wait, do we?"

"No," he said. "We don't."

She took his shoulders and pulled him along with her as she lay back on the hay. Their lips met and then parted for a deep, wet kiss. Buttermilk's body pressed against her, and involuntarily he began grinding his pelvis against hers. She responded and moaned low. She began to pull at his shirt, and he sat up on his knees to help her. It was off in an instant, and he reached for the front of her blouse. Soon that, too, was off and tossed aside, and Buttermilk marveled at the beauty of her round, firm breasts. He reached out and put a hand on each one and rubbed and kneaded gently. He leaned forward and kissed her again, then eased himself down lower to take a budding nipple into his mouth. He licked and sucked, and she groaned with intense pleasure.

She loved what he was doing to her, but she wanted more, so she pulled him upward by his shoulders, and when their lips met once again, she reached for the waistband of his trousers and began fumbling with his belt buckle. He rolled off her and onto his back. Then he pulled off his boots and his trousers. While he was busy with that, Felicia stood up and loosened her skirt, which she then let fall down around her ankles. She stepped out of it and tossed it aside with a foot. In another instant, Buttermilk lay naked, and Felicia stood over him fully undressed.

He looked up at her in wonder, barely able to catch his breath. She looked down at him, pleased to see that he was more than ready for her. She stepped over to straddle his knees, then knelt. Both her hands reached out to fondle his throbbing cock and stroke his heavy balls. He almost yelled out with the thrill of her touch. Then she leaned forward, her face close to his rod, and he could hardly believe what was about to happen to him. Her tongue shot out and licked his shaft. He flinched at the touch. She licked again, around and around, and then all at once, she took the head into her mouth. She slipped it out between tight lips, then took it in again. Buttermilk groaned out loud.

Felicia lowered her head, taking in the full length of his cock, and then she began moving up and down its length. He responded by thrusting gently. She took one last slow slurp, and then got up to her knees again. Moving forward, she lowered herself onto the stiff stalk until she was sitting on him with the whole length inside her wet pussy. "Ahhh," she moaned through a broad smile. Then she thrust her pelvis forward, sliding her ass cheeks along his upper thighs, then back again, slowly at first, then faster and faster. Feeling the powerful climax upon her, she cried out, "Oh, God," as surge after surge of intense pleasure flooded her entire body. She stopped rocking, shivered, and fell forward, her breasts against his chest, her wet, open lips pressing against his mouth.

She straightened herself up again, and she rode him again, and again, to climax after climax. Each time her shudders were more violent, her moans louder. Both their bodies were wet with sweat. Following her final come, she kissed Buttermilk again. "You want to get on top?" she whispered in his ear. "Oh yeah," he said. They held each other tight and rolled in the hay until he was on top, and then he began to drive his hard rod into her cunt. Almost desperate, he pounded into her, faster and harder with each thrust.

Then he felt the pressure building. He knew that he would not last much longer, but he no longer wanted it to last. He longed for the massive release. A low rumble escaped from his throat and grew louder with each furious thrust. Then he exploded into her depths, spurt after spurt flooding her deep inside. Spent at last, he lay heavily on her, breathing deeply.

"You're wonderful," she said.

"You are, too," he said. "There just ain't enough words to say it."

Slocum was awake and alert. He wasn't sure if Jimson was still awake, but Jimson was supposed to be on guard with him. He thought that if the old man had dropped off, it would be all right. He'd been through a lot these last few days, and Slocum was not about to chastise him for nodding off at his duty. The others were all asleep. Slocum watched the house. It was dark. They had put on no lights as the sun went down. He would have done the same thing. Keep it dark in there so the beseigers would not be able to see anyone moving about.

There was a full moon in the sky, throwing light onto one side of the house and casting eerie shadows in the yard from the trees. The wind picked up a little, and the shadows danced strange and macabre movements on the ground and against the side of the house. Slocum watched those movements carefully. They could have been designed to confuse the watchers. Once or twice he thought that he saw someone move there, only to discover that it was only the dancing shadows. Then he saw another suspicious motion. He squinted his eyes.

It was a man moving around from the back of the house. He was almost sure of it. He cranked the lever of his Winchester, loading a shell into the chamber. The noise startled Jimson. He jerked his head and popped open his eyes. "What is it, Slocum?" he asked in a harsh whisper.

"Someone moving around down there," said Slocum. "He seems to be coming our way."

"Trying to slip up on us in the dark, eh?" Jimson said.

"What do you want me to do about him?" Slocum asked.

"He's up to no good," Jimson said. "Drop him in his tracks."

"Okay," said Slocum, raising the rifle to his shoulder and managing to get a bead on the man in the dark. He watched for a moment, as the man seemed to dance on top of the front sight of the rifle, moving closer. He was running in a low crouch and holding a six-gun in his right hand. He came closer. Slocum squeezed the trigger. The man yowled and twisted and fell to the ground.

"Good shot," said Jimson. The other cowhands woke up, startled awake by the sound of the shot.

"I'm not so sure," Slocum said. "I think I just winged him is all."

"As long as it put him out of commission," said Jimson.

"What is it?" one of hands asked, scrambling up beside Jimson, gun in hand.

"It's okay," Slocum said. "One of them tried to sneak his way up here, but I stopped him. Go on back to sleep."

"Hell," said the cowhand, "I can't now."

As the wounded man staggered through the back door into the ranch house, Orwig met him there. "I'm hit," the man said.

"How bad?" Orwig asked.

"Shit," the man said, "bad enough. I'm bleeding like a stuck pig."

Orwig lit a lamp so he could inspect the damage. They were in a back room, and he was pretty sure that the Jimson bunch was all out front. It should be all right. He tore the man's shirt away from the wound and squinted at it.

"You'll live," he said, "if we can stop it from bleeding so damn much. Hold on. I'll get one of the boys to patch you up."

Orwig went through the door into the front room and called for help. He sent a man to tend to the wound. Then he paced among the others.

"Where the hell is Young?" he said at last. "Has anyone seen him lately?"

"Not him nor that One Shot," one said.

"You reckon they got shot?" another asked.

"I don't think so," Orwig said. "I think we'd know if they did. Besides, it ain't likely that they'd a both got hit and kilt."

"Well, they could be hiding out somewhere else," said one of the hands. "Maybe they went outside whenever we come in. Maybe we kind a crossed our paths, you know."

"Maybe," said Orwig. "I'd sure like to know where the hell they're at. We're in a tight spot here."

He started pacing again, and he banged a leg on the steel door of the safe. He cursed, then bent over to look at what it was he had run into. Even in dark, he could see that the safe door was standing wide open. He called into the back room. "Bring that light in here," he said.

"I got one right here," said one of the men. He struck a match and lit the lamp. He carried it over to Orwig, who took it and held it to the safe, looking wide-eyed into its emptiness.

"Cleaned out," he said.

"What?" said one of the men.

"They cleaned out the safe and run out on us is what they done," Orwig said. "The sons of bitches. They left us here to cover their ass while they're running out on us with all the money. Dirty, double-crossing bastards."

"Well, what'll we do?"

"I don't know," Orwig said. He stood up and started pacing again. "I don't know. Let me think. Damn it."

As the sun appeared on the horizon, Buttermilk and Felicia, with some instructions from Molly, finished loading the wagon. Buttermilk hitched the horses to the wagon and prepared to climb up onto the seat. Felicia took hold of him and embraced him.

"Buttermilk," she said, "I'm scared. Be careful."

He put his arms around her and held her close and tight for a moment. Then he kissed her tenderly. Molly watched with interest.

"Don't worry, darlin'," he said. "I mean to come back in one piece. I got too much at stake now. I ain't letting nothing keep me from marrying up with you."

"I love you," she said.

"I love you, too," he said. Then he pulled himself loose from her embrace. "I got to go right now though," he added.

"I know," she said. "Be careful."

"I'm coming back to you," he said. He climbed onto the seat, took up the reins, and gave them a flick to start the horses. As Felicia stood watching him drive off, Molly moved over to stand beside her. She put an arm around the younger woman's shoulders and gave her a hug.

"He's a fine young man," she said.

"He asked me to marry him," Felicia said.

"And what did you answer?" Molly asked.

"Oh, I said yes," Felicia said. "Yes. Molly, I'm so worried about him."

"I know," Molly said. "I know. My man's out there, too. All we can do is wait and hope for the best. And pray."

Buttermilk whipped up the horses. He was in a hurry to get back to Jimson and Slocum and the others. He had felt guilty about not going back the night before, but he had his orders from the boss, and they had been reinforced by the boss's lady. Then he'd had one of the greatest nights of his entire life, and that made him feel even more guilty. He hoped that everyone was all right over there. He knew that his sense of guilt was irrational. There were plenty of men over there. They were in a good position, and they had Slocum with them. Even so he was not comfortable with the fact that they had been out there all night, and he—well, he had not been.

True, they needed the supplies in the wagon in order to lay down an extended seige, and it would have been difficult to drive the wagon in the dark. He kept telling himself all those reasons, reasons why he should not be feeling bad, over and again. But then, he thought, maybe the only thing that was wrong was that they were out there for a fight, and even though they did not know, he knew, that he was in reality the Rock Port Kid. Someone else should have been sent for the supplies.

Slocum glanced at the sun peeking up over the edge of the horizon. He looked back toward the house. "We're going to have to do something soon," he said to Jimson. "We're going to need food and water, and we're getting low on ammunition."

"We've got supplies coming," Jimson said. "I think we'll hold out long enough for that."

"What do you intend to do anyhow?" Slocum asked. "Just wait them out?"

"For now," Jimson said, "that's my plan. Just what you said. Just wait them out."

14

Orwig saw that it would be daylight soon. He looked out a front window toward the men up on the rise at the front gate. He paced a bit, then turned to face the others in the room.

"Boys," he said, "I never thought it would come to this, but I suggest we give ourselves up."

"They'll hang us all," said one of the men.

"If we don't give ourselves up," Orwig said, "they'll kill us all for sure. If we surrender, they'll have to give us a trial, and they might not be able to prove that any of us done a killing. We might get off scot-free. You can't never tell, but I think our chances of surviving this thing will be better if we let them take us to trial."

He looked around the room. No one responded. Assuming that silence was assent, he walked over to the corner of the room where a mop leaned against the wall. Taking a white handkerchief out of his pocket, he tied it to the end of the mop handle and walked toward the door.

With the supply wagon behind them, all of Jimson's men had eaten their fill and had plenty of coffee. They had loaded all their guns full and had plenty more ammunition should they need it. They were ready for whatever might happen next, and all-out assault or a long siege. Everyone was back in position and watching the house. Jimson said to Slocum, "I think something's about to happen here."

"Why do you say that?" Slocum asked.

"It's just a feeling," said Jimson. "Call me crazy, but I think it's about to bust wide open."

"Well, you're right about one thing," Slocum said. "Something's happening all right. Look."

Jimson looked at the house and saw that the front door had been thrown open. He yelled out for all his men to hear, "Hold your fire, boys, till I give the word." In another moment a mop handle with a white flag tied on its end was poked out the door. "I'll be damned," he said. Then he raised his voice. "What do you want?" he called out.

"We want to come out and surrender," Orwig answered.

"Throw your guns out ahead of you," Jimson yelled.

"Be careful," said Slocum. "It could be some kind of trick."

"We'll watch them," Jimson said, as the first few guns were thrown out the door into the yard. More guns were tossed out. Then Orwig, still carrying the mop, stepped out in view.

"That's all of them," he said.

"Step on out into the yard," Jimson called. "All of you."

In a couple of minutes ten toughs were standing in a row in the yard in front of Young's house. Jimson counted them. He stood up. "Is that all of you?" he called to them.

"It's all," Orwig answered.

Slocum stood up and yelled out, "I don't see Young or Parsons down there."

"They run out on us," said Orwig.

Slocum and Jimson exchanged a glance. "What do you think?" Jimson asked.

"Only one way to find out," Slocum said. "Let's go on down and round them up."

"Boys," Jimson said, "there's two more of you than there are of them. I want each one of you to go down there and take charge of a prisoner. Watch him like a hawk. The extra two boys, you two check them all over for any weapons they might not have throwed out. When you're sure they ain't armed no more, get them mounted up and get their hands tied. We'll take them into town to the jailhouse."

As the cowhands started down toward the house, Jimson and Slocum watched from their vantage point in case of any surprises that might pop up. There were none. Soon the cowhands had the Young crew tied and mounted up. The small pile of weapons in front of the house had grown by a few knives and small pocket revolvers. Jimson had another cowhand give Buttermilk his horse and take the wagon back to the ranch. With the prisoners all securely tied, he decided that everyone could go back to the ranch with the exception of himself, Slocum, and Buttermilk. The three men then drove the twelve prisoners into Harleyville and locked them in the jail cells.

Slocum was standing out on the board sidewalk, and Jimson stepped out to join him. He pulled a rag out of his pocket and wiped the sweat off his brow. "I sure would like to know what come of Young and Parsons," he said. Then he saw Ed Harman, the bank president, coming toward him at a run. "Wonder what he's up to," he said.

The banker came running on up and stopped, breathing heavy to catch his breath.

"What is it, Ed?" Jimson asked.

"Is it true what I heard?" said Harman.

"Well, I don't know," said Jimson. "Just what did you hear?"

"That you been made marshal," said Harman.

"It's true enough," Jimson admitted. "Just long enough to clear up this mess with Parley Young."

"Well, you're not going to believe this," said Harman, "but Young and that gunfighter of his, that Parsons, came into town yesterday afternoon and robbed the bank."

"Well, I'll be damned," said Jimson. "There's no doubt about it? I mean, were they masked or anything like that?"

"No, they weren't," Harman said. "They just walked in big as you please, the two of them. Then Young said he wanted to withdraw all his money. After he had it all, the other one pulled out his gun and said he wanted to make a withdrawal, too. Young took out his gun, too, and they got a bunch of money. I haven't had time to calculate it all yet. They didn't clean us out. They were in too big a hurry. But they took enough. Several thousand, I'd say."

"Did anyone see which way they went?" Jimson asked.

"No," said Harman. "They said that if anyone stuck his head out the door they'd blow it off. We stayed still for a respectable period of time. When I finally peeked out, they were long gone."

"All right, Ed," said Jimson. "We'll take care of it. Go on back to the bank and get to calculating. We'll need to know just how much they got off with."

As Harman walked back toward the bank, Slocum said, "Well, that explains some things."

"I reckon it does," said Jimson. "They seen the writing on the wall and got out of here with as much as they could carry."

"Leaving those men in the jail to face us and hold us off," said Slocum.

"That's why those men went ahead and give up so easy," Jimson said. "They didn't have no boss telling them what to do."

"They didn't have anyone left around to pay them," Slocum said.

"Yeah," said Jimson.

"Well, what now?" Slocum asked.

"I don't think I can turn in my commission till Parley Young and that Parsons are behind bars," Jimson said.

"Or dead," said Slocum.

"Well, yeah," Jimson agreed.

"You got a jail full of prisoners in there," Slocum said, "and you got a town here that's been without a lawman for a while now. Why don't you let me and ole Buttermilk go after those two?"

"Ahh, I don't know," Jimson began, but Slocum cut him off short.

"You'll be needed around here," he said. "I've faced that kind before, and I know that—well, I feel pretty sure that

Buttermilk can stand up to the best of them."

"Buttermilk's a good man," Jimson said, "but I don't know about sending him out after a professional gun hand like that Parsons."

"Mr. Jimson," said Slocum, "I'm going to tell you something that I swore I'd keep to myself, so I want you to promise me you'll keep it to yourself, and you won't hold it against anyone."

Jimson gave Slocum a sideways look and studied him for a moment. "All right," he said. "You have my word."

"You ever hear of a young gunslinger called the Rock Port Kid?" Slocum asked him.

"Just about everyone's heard about the Rock Port Kid," said Jimson. "He just kind of disappeared a couple of years ago, didn't he?"

"Just a little while before Buttermilk showed up around here, wouldn't you say?" Slocum asked.

"Say," said Jimson, "you ain't trying to tell me that Buttermilk Smith is—"

"The Rock Port Kid," said Slocum. "Can me and him go after Parsons and Young?"

"Well," said Jimson. "I'd a never thought it. Well, yeah. I guess you can."

Parley Young and Aaron Parsons rode into a little town called Drinkwater. It was a sleepy town without too much traffic. It had a saloon, a general store, a couple of eating establishments, a small hotel, a livery stable, and a few other small business establishments on a short main street. The two men were dirty, tired, hungry, and thirsty. They had ridden all night and half the next day. The sun was high in the sky.

Taking the lead, Parsons pulled up in front of a small eatery. Dismounting, he looked at a young boy standing on the sidewalk. As Young dismounted, Parsons took the reins of both horses in his hands and spoke to the boy. "Take care of these horses," he said, "and I'll give you a dollar."

"A dollar?" the boy said.

"That's right," said Parsons. "Take them over to the stable and tell the man to look after them real good."

He dug into a pocket as he handed the reins to the boy.
Then he dropped the dollar into the boy's open hand.

"Thanks, mister," the boy said, heading for the stable and
tugging on the reins. Parsons pulled the saddlebags off as
his horse moved past him, then turned and headed into the
eatery, followed by Young. Inside, they ordered steak dinners and coffee. "Water first," said Parsons. They drank the
water greedily, and when their meals arrived, ate them as
if they were starving. They finished up with several cups
of coffee each. Young paid for the food, and they walked
over to the saloon. Parsons got a bottle and two glasses,
and they sat at a table. They lit cigars and drank.

"Aaron," said Young, "do you think we're far enough
away from Harleyville to stop for the night?"

"I figure we got at least a day and a half on them,"
Parsons said. "We'll put up here for the night. Rest our
horses and ourselves. Then we'll get us an early start in the
morning. We'll head west."

"Well, how come," said Young, "if we're going west,
how come we been headed north all this time?"

"To throw them off, you dumb ass," Parsons said. "If
they're lucky enough, or good enough, to track us to this
dump, they'll have it in their heads that we're going north.
They'll keep on that way."

"Oh," said Young. He lifted his glass and took another
drink. "You got anyplace in particular in mind?"

"California gold country," Parsons said. "There're lots of
men there. It'll be easy to get lost. Then too, there's lots
of action. We got plenty enough to last us awhile, so I
figure we'll just take it easy for a spell. But when we're
ready, like I said, there's lots of action out that way."

"Okay," said Young. "Sounds good to me."

After a couple more drinks, Parsons stoppered the bottle.
As he stood up, he said to Young, "Bring that along." He
headed for the front door. Young grabbed the bottle and
followed Parsons across the street to the small hotel. The
lobby inside was close and dingy. A bald-headed man was
behind the counter. A tired-looking whore lounged in a

stuffed chair across the room. Parsons looked at her, then walked on to the counter.

"We need a couple of rooms," he said.

He paid the man and registered, then added, "And a bath."

"Two baths," said Young.

"It'll take a little while," the man said.

"Then I suggest you get to it," Parsons said. He nodded toward the woman across the room and said, "Is she for hire?"

"Yeah," the man said.

"Send her up with the bath," said Parsons. "We'll be leaving in the morning. Early. What do I owe you for everything?"

He settled again, took two room keys, and tossed one to Young. Then he headed for the stairs. Finding the rooms, he opened one door and looked in. Then he opened the other room and checked it over. Nodding to the second room and handing Young a key, he said, "You take that one." Then he went inside the first room. He tossed his saddlebags on the bed. Young's pockets were stuffed with the money he had taken from his own safe and from his own bank account, but Parsons had all of the stolen bank money in the saddlebags. He had no idea which was the largest amount.

He took off his coat and hat and pulled off his boots. Unbuckling his gun belt, he rebuckled it and hung it on the headboard of the bed. Then he stretched himself out on the bed to wait for his bath and his whore. He thought about all the money that Young had on him, and he wondered if he would want Young around for anything much longer. It would be easy to kill the son of a bitch and take all the money. He asked himself why he didn't go ahead and do that. Not in town though, he told himself. Tomorrow would be soon enough. Tomorrow out on the trail. There would be no witnesses. Maybe no one would ever even find the body. Then, with all the money, Parsons figured that he would be well set up for a good long time.

A tub was brought into the room and several buckets of

hot water were poured into it. A small table was set by the tub with wash rag, towel, and soap on it. The whore from downstairs came into the room. The man who had set up the bath left. "Close the door," Parsons said. She closed it and latched it. Parsons started to undress. She did the same. "What's your name?" he asked her.

"Meg," she said.

"Meg," he said, "I want you to wash me—all over."

Naked, with half a hard-on, he stepped over the edge into the tub and settled himself down in the hot water with a heavy sigh. Meg knelt beside the tub and picked up the soap. She dipped the soap into the water and started to rub it on Parsons's chest. "You got a nice hairy chest," she said. "I like a man with a hairy chest."

"Yeah," he said. "Scrub lower. There's more hair down there."

Meg plunged her arm down into the water and found his eager rod. She began to stroke it with the soap, and Parsons began to thrust into her fist. Soon water was sloshing out of the tub, and Parsons was humping eagerly. Then he shouted with sudden release, and even under the hot water, Meg could feel the sticky substance run down his rod and onto her hand. Parsons relaxed with a long sigh.

"Climb in," he said. "The water's fine."

Meg got into the tub with Parsons, and she soon had lathered them both all over. They stood up together, and she took the towel and dried him off. Then as he moved over to the bed, she dried herself. Dropping the towel, she looked at him. "What do you want me to do?" she said.

"Come on over here," he said.

She walked over to the bed and crawled in beside him. He reached a hand down between her thighs and probed for the warm, wet slit. Finding it, he began to stroke, and she began to moan and roll her hips. In another moment, Parsons was hard again. "Turn over," he said. "Get up on your hands and knees. I'm going to fuck you like a dog."

Meg assumed the position, thrusting her round ass out for him. On his knees, he moved in behind her. She reached between her legs and took hold of his cock, guiding it into the squishy hole. He thrust forward hard, slapping his own thighs and belly against her ass. His heavy balls swung back and forth as he plunged into her again and again.

"Oh. Oh. Oh," she said. "Oh, you're so big. So hard."

"I'm going to fuck you to death, baby," he said, ramming his rod into her over and over.

He paused to catch his breath, and he pulled her ass hard against him. She wriggled her hips against him, feeling his cock move against the sides of her cunt. Then he began driving again. Suddenly he pulled out and turned her on her back. He flopped down on her and drove his cock into her hole again. Lying between her legs, on her belly, he humped hard and fast. His breathing was fast and loud and heavy. She moaned and twittered.

"Oh, God, you're good," she said.

"I'm the best you've ever had," he said.

"Yeah," she said, "you're the best."

Then with no warning, he pulled out of her and straightened himself up. He was upright but still on his knees between her legs. He took hold of his cock with his right hand and began pumping it and moaning. She watched with astonishment as he jerked his cock faster and faster. His eyes glazed over. He moaned deep in his chest. Then a shot came out of his cock, and the warm, sticky juice hit her on the left titty.

"Oh," she said.

He fired another shot and another. They landed between her tits and on her belly, and the last few dribbled down into her pubic hairs. Spent, he sighed and fell back onto his back. Meg rubbed the fresh come over her skin like a salve.

15

Slocum and Buttermilk rode out early in the morning. They had started the day by questioning folks in Harleyville. Finally they found someone who was sure that two men had ridden out of town headed north just about the time the bank had been robbed. It was the best clue they had. They decided to ride north. They knew that Parsons and Young had a good headstart on them. From what they could gather from the prisoners in the Harleyville jail, Parsons and Young had slipped away the evening the seige had been laid down at the Young ranch. If that were indeed the case, that meant that the two fugitives had been out on the trail for two nights and a day by the time Slocum and Buttermilk started after them. Of course, it was unlikely they had been riding that whole time. Slocum speculated that since they had sneaked off late in the evening, they might have ridden all that night and some into the next day. They would have had to have stopped during that day though. Somewhere.

"Do you know where the next town is?" he asked Buttermilk.

"It'd be Drinkwater," Buttermilk said. "It's at least a day's ride straight ahead."

"Likely they stopped there for a rest," Slocum said. "We'll find out when we get there."

They rode at a steady pace, taking care not to wear down their horses. They were silent for a space. Then Buttermilk spoke up. "When we find them, Slocum," he said, "what do you mean to do?"

"We promised Jimson that we'd try to bring them back alive for trial," Slocum said. "We'll try to keep that promise." He paused for a while before adding, "I hope that Young and Parsons don't let us keep it."

Buttermilk grinned. "I understand you," he said. "Bastards ain't worth putting on trial. Be a lot easier too than escorting their asses all the way back."

"We haven't found them yet," Slocum said.

"We will," Buttermilk said. "I ain't going back till we get them, one way or the other."

They rode the rest of that day without incident. With nightfall, they stopped and made a camp. They had packed supplies in with them, so they built a fire, cooked a meal, and boiled a pot of coffee. After they had finished the meal, they sat drinking coffee. Slocum lit a cigar. They were making small talk, when they heard the sound of an approaching horse.

"Get back out of the light," Slocum said. Buttermilk, taking his coffee cup with him, moved into the darkness away from the fire. The hoofbeats came closer. Then they stopped, and a voice came out of the darkness. "Hello, the camp. Can a traveler ride in?"

"Come on in, stranger," Slocum said.

The horse and rider moved into view. Slocum had never seen the man before. The man swung out of his saddle. "Name's Joe Morton," he said. "Traveling south. I was thinking about finding me a campsite for the night when I seen your fire. Can you stand some company?"

"Put your horse over there with my two," Slocum said, "and park yourself here at the fire. I've still got some hot food, and I've got plenty of coffee."

"Thanks," said Morton. He led his horse over next to Slocum's and Buttermilk's. If he was curious about the two horses, he kept quiet about it. He walked back over to the fire and took a seat. Slocum handed him a cup full of steaming coffee. Morton took a slurp. "Sure is good," he said. Slocum took note that Morton was not packing a six-gun.

"Buttermilk," he said, "come on in."

Morton looked up surprised as Buttermilk walked back into the light of the fire.

"Howdy," said Buttermilk.

Morton smiled. "Being cautious, I see," he said. "Not a bad idea these days."

Slocum handed Morton a dish of food.

"Thanks again," Morton said, and he began eating like a man who was hungry. Buttermilk sat down so that the three men made a triangle around the fire.

"You ride through Drinkwater?" he asked.

"Yep," Morton said.

"How long ago?"

"Left out of there about noon," said Morton. "That where you're headed?"

"That's right," Slocum said.

"Well," said Morton, "you get started early, you'd oughta be there by noon tomorrow."

"We're looking for a couple of men," Slocum said. "One of them will be wearing black. Wearing his guns low. You didn't happen to see them up there, did you?"

"By God, I sure did," Morton said. "I seen that one in black for sure. I think there was another man with him, but I didn't hardly notice him. I sure did notice that one in black though. Yes sir. Someone told me he was known as One Shot. A good one to steer clear of. That's what the man said."

"Do you know if he was still in town when you left?" Slocum asked.

"Know he was," Morton said. "I seen him on the sidewalk as I was riding out. You can't miss that feller. He stands out in a crowd. Yes sir."

Slocum and Buttermilk exchanged a quick glance. If Young and Parsons had not yet left Drinkwater, they were only a half day's ride ahead. On the other hand, if they had ridden out shortly after Morton had, they could be a full day ahead. At least they knew that were on the right trail— so far.

Young and Parsons were sitting at a table in the saloon. Parsons poured them each a drink. He lifted his own glass and took a sip, then put the glass down again. "Young," he said, "we got to pull out of here in the morning. We done laid around here too long for comfort already. If anyone's on our trail, they'll likely be headed right on up here. Early in the morning, we'll head west."

"Whatever you say, Aaron," Young said. He was thinking of the irony in their situation. He was the one who had hired Parsons in the first place, because he had felt the need for a professional gunfighter, a slick and feared one. Then things had turned on him, and now that they were fugitives, Parsons had assumed the role of boss. He was making all the decisions and giving all the orders. Young did not like that, but he was afraid of Parsons. He knew that the man could kill him in a heartbeat, and would if provoked or even if it should suddenly become expedient. He was fast, efficient, and cold-blooded. Young felt like he was in a very precarious position, and one from which he could see no way at present of extricating himself.

He did want to get away from this man though, and as soon as possible. He thought about all the money they had between them. He had all his own money, but Parsons had the money from the bank robbery. Well, let him keep it. He had enough of his own, and it was well worth letting Parsons keep the bank's money, if it meant that he could keep his life. He finished his drink and stood up.

"I think I'll turn in," he said, "so I'll be ready to go in the morning."

Parsons waved him away, and Young left the saloon. He walked back to his room in the hotel and packed his things. Then he sat up and waited. He waited at least an hour and was beginning to feel nervous and impatient, but at last he heard the sound of footsteps in the hallway. He heard a woman giggling, too, and then he heard the voice of Aaron Parsons. He waited, tense. He could tell when Parsons

opened the door to his room, and when he shut it again.
He sat still—listening.

It didn't take long. The sounds coming through the wall
were unmistakable. Parsons was involved in his fun, and
likely he would be occupied for some time. Young picked
up his bundle and walked easily to his door. He opened it
slowly and carefully. The hallway looked especially long
to him as he moved toward the stairs, afraid with every step
that in spite of his current preoccupation Parsons would
hear him and come out into the hall. He did not, and Young
made it to the head of the stairway. He looked back over
his shoulder three times before he made it to the ground
floor. Then he hurried outside and on over to the stable.

At the stable, he woke the liveryman up and had him
saddle his horse. He tied on his bundle, paid the man, and
climbed into the saddle. He knew that Parsons would kill
him if they ever crossed paths again, and he knew that
Parsons intended to head west. He decided to ride south for
a few miles, the last direction Parsons would expect him to
go. They both expected that someone, maybe even a posse,
would be coming from Harleyville. Young thought that he
could ride south a few miles in the darkness, then turn east
before he met up with the posse. Parsons would not be
looking either south or east. And even if Young were to
meet the posse or whoever was riding out from Harleyville,
he figured he'd be better off with them than with Parsons.
He rode hard.

With the light of day, Buttermilk, Slocum, and Morton
crawled out of their bedrolls. They built up the campfire
and fixed breakfast and coffee. When they were finished
with it, they cleaned up the campsite. Morton thanked them
for their hospitality, they thanked him for the information
he had given them, and they rode off in two different directions. Riding along side by side, Slocum and Buttermilk
were silent. Both men were thinking of their prey. They
might meet up with them by noon in Drinkwater, or they
might discover that the two fugitives had already left. If
that were the case, they would have to try to discover which

direction they had ridden when they left town.

Buttermilk was especially anxious to get this job done. He was longing for the company of Felicia, and he was just itching to set a wedding date. He wasn't at all sure what he was going to do about a house for himself and his new wife, but that was just one more reason he wanted to get this unpleasant job over with. He needed to get back and look for a place to live. He was craving married life with Felicia. Now and then he felt like expressing these thoughts out loud, but he kept his mouth shut. He figured if he said anything about his concerns back home, Slocum would tell him to turn around and go back. He would just keep it to himself.

Parsons woke up early and took his time dressing. It was early enough that he figured he could afford the time. He thought about rousting Young out, but then he told himself he didn't give a damn if Young got any breakfast before they hit the trail. If Young slept late, that would be Young's problem. Parsons went across the street to one of the eateries and had himself a good breakfast. Done with it, he had two more cups of coffee. Then he walked back to his room in the hotel. It was time to hit the trail. He packed his stuff up, then went out into the hall and banged on the door of Young's room. There was no answer. He banged again. Finally, he tried the door and found it unlocked. He also found the room empty.

He cursed and hurried downstairs and on over to the stable. Then he discovered the truth. Young had pulled out on him the night before. He cursed again, more vilely than the first time. He had fully meant to kill Young someplace out on the trail and take all the money for himself. He thought about pursuing Young, but he had no way of knowing which direction to take. The weasley son of a bitch could have gone off in any direction—except south, of course. Only a fool would head back toward Harleyville after having been seen robbing the bank there. Young was lots of things, but Parsons did not think him to be a fool.

Well, he decided, there was nothing for it but to be satisfied with his bank loot and stick to his own original plan, which was to head west for California. He mounted up and started out of town. It was going to be a long and lonely ride, but he had plenty of money to use each time he came to a town.

For the first several miles of his ride out of Drinkwater, Parley Young kept looking over his shoulder in case Parsons should be on his trail. Finally he relaxed a bit. He knew that he would still have to be vigilant. He would have to watch behind him and ahead of him. Behind for Parsons, ahead for any pursuit from Harleyville. His intention was to turn east at some convenient location, but he wanted a road or at least a well-traveled trail to ride. He did not want to just head east across the country. There would be no way of knowing how far it would be to any kind of civilization that way, and Young was no frontiersman. On the other hand, he did not want to delay his turn off for too long. He did not want to meet up with a posse from Harleyville.

Slocum and Buttermilk had just topped a rise, when Slocum reined in his big Appaloosa. "Hold up," he said to Buttermilk. "Move off the road." The two riders moved to the side where they would not as easily be seen.

"What is it?" Buttermilk said.

"Look down there," said Slocum. "Rider. Just heading off east. Does he look familiar?"

"It's a long look," Buttermilk said. "Just a minute."

He reached into his saddlebag and brought out a pair of binoculors. Raising them to his eyes, he sighted in on the rider. "It's Parley Young, all right," he said.

"They've split up," Slocum said.

"What do we do?" Buttermilk asked. "Go after Young?"

"It'd take us a while to catch up with him," Slocum said, "and all the while, Parsons will be putting more territory between him and us. Why don't you go after Young and let me keep on the trail of Parsons?"

"Parsons is a hell of a gunfighter, Slocum," said Buttermilk. "Do you think you can handle him? I know the Rock Port Kid can take him."

"That's a good point," said Slocum. "But I think I can deal with him all right. If we have to split up, I'd rather do it this way. I'd rather you get back to the ranch as soon as you can. Fill Jimson in on what's happening. Take care of that gal of yours."

"Slocum," said Buttermilk, "I came out on this hunt with you of my own will. I don't need no special favors, just 'cause—"

"The favor's not for you," Slocum said. "If it's a favor at all, it's for her. But it's not that really. I figure you, being one of Jimson's hands, got a special score to settle with ole Young. Parsons is just a hired gun. He wouldn't even be around these parts if Young hadn't sent for him. I thought you might want to deal with the more personal part and let me take the other one. The impersonal one."

"I think you're trying to pull some shit on me, Slocum," said Buttermilk, "but I won't argue no more. We're wasting time."

"Good," said Slocum. "Be seeing you."

He urged his big horse forward, and just after, Buttermilk moved out at an angle toward the rider in the distance. Moving on ahead toward Drinkwater, Slocum felt good. He knew that Buttermilk could take Young easily. Then he would head on home. He would be safe, and he would be back with Felicia. Buttermilk might have been right about the Rock Port Kid being able to take One Shot, but Slocum wasn't totally sure of that, and he didn't want anything to happen to the kid. This way, he would put the kid and Young out of his mind, figuring that it was a done deal. He would concentrate on his own chore, that of running down and capturing, or killing, One Shot. He rode ahead.

As Joe Morton had predicted, Slocum arrived in Drinkwater around noon. He stopped in front of the saloon and went inside to order a whiskey. At the bar, he gave the bartender a description of Aaron Parsons and asked if he had seen the man.

"Yeah," the barkeep said. "He was in here. I ain't seen him since yesterday."

"Do you know if he's still in town?" Slocum asked.

The bartender shrugged. "I ain't seen him since yesterday," he said.

Slocum finished his drink and went back outside. There was a hotel across the road. He decided to try that. He walked across the street and went outside. There was a bald-headed man behind the counter. Slocum walked over to the counter, and the man looked up.

"You want a room?" he asked.

"That depends," Slocum said. "I'm looking for someone. Friend of mine. His name's Parsons. He usually dresses in black and wears his guns slung low. He was traveling with another fellow."

"You're too late," the man said. "They're done gone. Early this morning."

"Thanks," Slocum said, and he left the hotel. He stood for a while on the sidewalk, thinking. If Young and Parsons had both left early, the chances were that not too many people were around to see which way they had ridden out of town. He knew, of course, that Young had ridden south and then cut off the trail to head east. Obviously, the two had parted company, but which way then had Parsons gone? If they had stabled their horses, there was a chance that the liveryman might have noticed.

He found the livery in short order. Drinkwater wasn't much of a town. He walked in and found the man asleep. "Hey, pardner," he said. The man snorted. "Hey, wake up," Slocum said, a little louder. The man opened his eyes and looked up at Slocum.

"What the hell can I do for you?" he said.

"I'm looking for a man who rode out of here early this morning," Slocum said. "A gunfighter, dressed in black wearing low-slung guns."

"I recall a feller like that," the man said.

"Do you recall when he rode out of here?"

"Like you said, early this morning. It was still dark. He woke me up, too."

"Did you notice which way he rode out of town?" Slocum asked.

"Nope," the man said. "Soon as he climbed on his horse, I went back to sleep."

"Thanks anyhow," said Slocum, and he turned to walk back out to the street.

"Wait a minute, mister," the liveryman said. "I know someone who might be able to help you out."

Slocum turned back to face the man again. "Who might that be?" he asked.

The man walked to his front door and pointed to the eatery across the street. "Sam over there," he said. "He's up early getting ready for his breakfast customers. He mighta seen something."

"Thanks," said Slocum, and he walked across to the eatery. It was lunchtime, so the place was busy. Slocum took a chair at an empty table. Soon a man in a greasy apron came over to the table.

"What'll it be, mister?" he said.

"You tell me," Slocum said.

"Beef stew," said the man.

By the time Slocum had eaten his beef stew and had a couple of cups of coffee, the crowd was thinning out. The man came back to his table with the coffeepot.

"Want some more?" he asked.

"No thanks," Slocum said. "Are you Sam?"

"Yeah," Sam said. "How come?"

"The man over at the livery said you might have noticed my friend Parsons ride out of town early this morning. He wears black and carries his guns low."

"I seen him ride out headed west," said Sam.

When Buttermilk started riding after Parley Young, he thought it would be a quick chase. It didn't take him long to realize that the distance was greater than he had anticipated. It was going to take longer to catch up with the man. He didn't want to ride too hard and fast. He would wear out his horse. He noticed that the country, moving east, was desolate. It might not be easy finding water. He'd have to take care in this pursuit. Several times, he lost sight of his prey, but when he once again spotted him, he took out his binoculars for another look. The good thing was that he was pretty sure that Young was unaware that he was being followed.

The bad thing was that he discovered that he was riding away the day. He wondered if Young would stop for the night. If so, he wondered if he would be able to keep moving in the darkness in order to close the gap. In the meantime, he just kept plodding along.

16

Using his glasses again, Buttermilk could see that Young was riding toward a tree line in the distance. Trees might mean water. As the sun was getting low in the sky, it also might mean that Young would make a camp there for the night. If he didn't, Buttermilk thought, he would be a fool. That is, unless he did know that Buttermilk was on his trail, in which case, he might continue into the darkness to keep some distance between them. Buttermilk did not think, however, that Young knew he was back there on the trail. He kept moving slow and easy. He didn't want to give Young any notion that he or anyone else was back there.

It was twilight by the time Young reached the trees. Buttermilk stopped and used his glasses again to watch. Sure enough, Young unsaddled his horse and started in on the business of establishing a camp. Buttermilk moved the glasses around, searching the area around Young. The trees appeared to be lining the bank of a stream of some kind. He decided that he would wait a bit and let Young get well settled in. The darkness would settle in, too, and then he could more easily move in on the camp and take Young by surprise. He rode easily a little while longer and then stopped to wait.

• • •

Parley Young had built himself a fire against the chill of the night air, but he had no food or coffee. He was hungry, but all he could do was get water from the stream. The water was good. It quenched his thirst, but once he had drunk his fill, he began to crave coffee, and food, and whiskey. He had no idea how far it would be to any sign of civilization, and he began to feel panic set in. He could starve to death out here. He had been in such a hurry to get away from Aaron Parsons that he had not taken the proper precautions. He should at least have packed some food and water. And coffee. Coffee would taste good. Whiskey, too. He made himself a place to sleep, but it was uncomfortable, and he was too hungry to sleep. He cursed himself and tried to sleep, but to no avail.

It was full dark, but Buttermilk could tell where Young was camped by the flickering campfire light. He moved ahead cautiously. Closer to the light in the trees, he dismounted and led his horse. At last, he was close enough for conversation. He stopped. He knew that Young would be no match for him in a gunfight, but in the darkness, sneaking in on any man's camp could be dangerous. He thought that he could see the form of a man lying down on the far side of the fire, but he could not be sure. Even if the form really was Young sacked out for the night, he might not be asleep, and he might have a gun in his hand. There was also the old trick of padding a bedroll and then moving out away from the light. Buttermilk was not about to fall for any of that.

"Parley Young," he said, "is that you?"

Young rolled quickly and scrambled into the darkness. Buttermilk lost sight of him. Damn it, he thought. I could have moved right in there and taken him. But now both men were in darkness, hidden from one another. Buttermilk moved to his own left, slipping his Colt out of the holster. At the same time, he moved closer to the fire and to the trees.

"Young," he called out, "I don't want to kill you. All I want is to take you back to Harleyville."

"To hang?" Young shouted from somewhere in the trees.

"That ain't up to me," Buttermilk said. "There'd be a trial."

"Well, I ain't going."

"Well, if you don't agree to go back with me," Buttermilk said, "I will kill you. That's for certain."

"I might kill you," Young said, and he fired a shot. Buttermilk could not tell where the shot went, only that it did not hit him. Young was apparently trying to tell where Buttermilk might be by the sound of his voice. Buttermilk moved to his own right and passed by the fire. Then he started moving forward. Soon he was in the trees. He thought that Young was on the other side of the fire from him.

"You won't kill me like that," he said, and Young fired again. Buttermilk pressed himself against a tree trunk and looked around it. Everything was dark except a small circle around the glowing fire. He could see Young's saddle there, and he could see his blanket. But something seemed wrong. Something was missing. Then it came to him. He saw nothing to indicate that a meal had been prepared. He saw no coffeepot. This was not a full camp. It was just a place to sleep and get some water.

"You getting hungry, Young?" he called out.

He was answered by another shot from Young's revolver. "Fuck you," Young shouted.

"I've got some beans," said Buttermilk. "A slab of bacon, some biscuits. They're kind of hard, but they're tasty. I got coffee, too. It don't look to me like you had your supper. Did you?"

There was a long silence before Young answered.

"You promise you won't shoot me?" he said.

"Throw your gun out there by the fire where I can see and then come on out with your hands up," Buttermilk said.

"I don't know."

"How far you going to get without no food?" Buttermilk asked. "You even got a canteen? You want to starve to

death out here? Die of thirst? Toss out your gun, and I'll
have you a meal and hot coffee here in no time."

A revolver thudded in the dirt near the fire. In another
moment, Young stepped into view, his hands held high.

"Don't shoot me," he said. "I'm unarmed now. Don't
shoot."

Buttermilk stepped into the circle of light from the other
side of the fire. He picked the revolver up and tucked it
into the waistband of his trousers. Then he moved in closer
to Young.

"Turn around," he said, and Young did. Buttermilk patted him down to see if there were any hidden weapons. He
found none. "Stay right there in the light where I can see
you," he said. "I'm going out to get my horse."

Soon he was back at the camp. He unloaded and unsaddled his horse, then sent it toward the water with a slap on
the rump. He reached into his pack and pulled out a biscuit,
which he tossed to Young. Young caught it and began eating ravenously. Buttermilk kept unpacking. He came out
with a coffeepot, and looked up at Young. Young had
stuffed the last of his biscuit into his mouth. Buttermilk
said, "Here," and he tossed the pot at Young. Young caught
it.

"Go fill that up with water," Buttermilk said, "and we'll
boil up some coffee."

Young hurried off toward the stream. In a short while,
Buttermilk had prepared the meal and the coffee, and both
men had eaten their fill. They were sitting across the fire
from one another drinking coffee. Young felt much better
with his belly full, and much bolder. He was unarmed
though, and he knew better than to try to pull anything on
Buttermilk under those conditions. He decided to try another angle.

"Say, cowboy," he said, "how come you want to take
me back anyhow?"

"It's my job," Buttermilk said.

"A man can quit a job anytime," Young said, "and then
go get another job."

"I like my job, and I ain't got another one waiting for me."

"I could give you a job," Young said. "It wouldn't hardly be no work, and it would pay a hell of a lot better than the one you got right now. Hell, right now, it'd pay you better'n what you make in a year. Cash money."

"You got that kind of cash on you?" Buttermilk asked.

"I got it," said Young. "And I'll give it to you to just give me some food and coffee and a canteen. Give me back my gun and ride on out of here and leave me be. That's all you have to do."

"That don't sound too good to me," Buttermilk said. "I'd be out of a job too soon. I think I'll just stick with the job I got. Besides, that money you're talking about—it wouldn't be some of that stolen bank money, would it?"

"It's my money," Young said. "All legitimate. I never robbed that bank. It was Parsons done that. All I done was to just withdraw my own money out of the bank. Parsons pulled a gun and done the robbery. He's got all that bank money."

"That ain't the way they told it at the bank," Buttermilk said. "They say that the two of you robbed the bank together."

"It might'a looked that way to them, 'cause we went in there together, but I never knew that he was going to do that. He surprised me as much as them. I'm telling you the truth about that."

"How come you two split up anyhow?" Buttermilk asked.

"I was afraid that he was planning to kill me," Young said. "Take all my money, too. I sneaked off from him in the middle of the night. He's a cold-blooded son of a bitch."

"You hired him," said Buttermilk. "It was you that brought him in on this deal."

"That was a mistake," Young said. "I thought I needed professional help against that Slocum. I didn't know how bad Parsons was till it was too late."

Buttermilk saw that Young had finished his coffee. "You want another cup?" he asked.

"I've had enough," Young said.

"Okay," said Buttermilk, standing up. He pulled a length of rope out of his pack and walked around behind Young. "Put your hands behind your back," he said. Young did, and Buttermilk tied them. Then he dragged Young's bedroll over close to him. "Sleep well," he said. As Young stretched himself out on the blanket, Buttermilk unrolled his own and soon settled down for a good night's sleep.

Slocum rode a long, lonely trail. He came across no travelers and no homesteads. He did find a campsite once, abandoned. There was no way he could tell if it had been made by Aaron Parsons, although it seemed recent enough that it could have been. He rode on. He had nothing to go on except the word of the greasy cook in Drinkwater that Parsons had left town headed west. He rode the day away and stopped at night to camp. He fixed himself a meal and went to sleep.

Early the next morning, Slocum ate again, drank some coffee, cleaned up his campsite, and started back on the trail. About midmorning he came to a small town called Dog Trot. He made the usual inquiries and found out that Parsons had indeed passed through the day before. He had not seemed to be in a hurry. He also found out that there was another town not too far away. Parsons could have made it by nightfall. He could have spent the night in a hotel room while Slocum was sleeping on the trail. The name of the town was Cow Creek. Slocum watered his horse and rode on out of Dog Trot.

He stopped again at high noon to fix himself another meal. As soon as he was done, he broke camp and moved on out. By midafternoon, he could see Cow Creek ahead. If Parsons had decided that he had eluded any pursuit and was taking it easy, he might still be there. Slocum would have to be ready for anyone riding into the town. He let the big horse walk along at its own pace.

Moving into Cow Creek, Slocum watched all around. It was small and not busy. If Parsons was there, he would be easy to spot. On the other hand, if Parsons was hidden and watching out some window, he would just as easily spot Slocum riding into town. Slocum stopped in front of a small cantina. He dismounted and lapped the reins of his Appaloosa around the hitching rail. Then he went inside. This time he ordered himself a whiskey. Then he made his inquiry. Again, he was told that the man he hunted had passed through some hours ago. Slocum sighed. He decided that he would stick around Cow Creek long enough for a meal cooked by someone else, then get back on the trail.

A young man standing at the bar had overheard Slocum asking after Parsons. He finished his drink and then casually walked out the front door. He mounted his horse and rode out of town easily—heading west. Once out of town, he kicked his horse into a dead run. He was in a hurry. He rode his horse fast as long as he dared, then slowed the pace. After the horse was rested enough, he kicked it into a run again. He rode this way for a good part of the day. It was getting late in the evening. The sun was low in the sky. The rider saw up ahead a man in black riding down the road. He yelled and waved. The rider in black stopped, turned, and took a rifle out of a scabbard. He chambered a shell and raised the rifle.

The young man slowed his horse and stopped it, raising his own arms above his head.

"Mr. Parsons," he called out, "it's me. Rodney Trump. From Cow Creek. Remember? I got some news for you. Don't shoot."

Parsons lowered his rifle.

"Ride on over, Trump," he called.

Rodney Trump rode easy now, keeping his hands at about shoulder level. Parsons still held his rifle, but he held it casually. When Trump came in close enough for talk, Parsons said, "What news?"

"A man came into Cow Creek asking after you," Trump said. "I never caught his name. Don't think he ever give it. He said he was looking for a friend of his, but I never fell for that. He looked to me like he'd been on the trail for a spell. Big man. Tough-looking."

"That the best description you can give me?" Parsons said.

"He has the look of a cowhand," Trump said, "but I think he has the look of a gunman, too. Something about the way he carried his Colt. He's wearing jeans and a red shirt. White hat. Oh yeah. I ain't sure, but whenever I left, I seen a big Appaloosa tied out front. It musta been his. Hadn't no one else come in."

"Slocum," said Parsons. "Rodney, my boy, how would you like to make fifty bucks?"

"Oh, yes sir," Trump said. "What do you want me to do?"

"Ride along with me for a ways," Parsons said. "I'll tell you about it."

They rode in silence for a few miles. Then they came to a place in the road where the road had been cut through some small hills. Ahead, a large pile of boulders was off to the right side of the road. Parsons stopped and so did Trump.

"See that pile of rocks up there?" Parsons asked.

"Sure," said Trump. "I see them."

"Ride over there," said Parsons. "Take your horse back out of sight. Then take your rifle and hide yourself in amongst them rocks. When you see that son of a bitch come riding down this road, knock him out of the saddle."

"You mean, kill him?" Trump asked.

"Dead," said Parsons.

"Shoot him from ambush," said Trump. "Just like that?"

"I'll make it a hundred," Parsons said. "What do you say?"

"Yes sir," said Trump. "I'll do it."

Parsons pulled some bills out of his pocket and counted some out. Then he handed them to Trump. "Don't miss," he said, "or I'll come looking for you to get my money back."

"Don't worry, Mr. Parsons," Trump said. "I'm a dead shot with a rifle. I won't miss."

"Go on then," Parsons said. He watched for a moment as Trump headed for the boulders. Then he urged his own mount ahead. He told himself that he was not afraid to face Slocum. He just didn't want to be bothered. He wanted to move on ahead along the trail to the California gold-mining towns. He didn't want anyone bothering him or anything interfering with his plans. One hundred was little enough to eliminate an annoyance like Slocum.

17

The day was plenty hot and Slocum was riding slowly,
taking it easy on both himself and his horse. Up ahead and
off to one side of the narrow road was a large pile of boulders. It was an unusual formation along this particular road,
and largely for the relief of his eyes from the boredom, he
studied it as he moved along. He was looking at the strange
pile of rocks when he thought he detected a slight motion
in the shadows. It might have been a bird or a small animal,
even a trick of the shadows from the clouds in the sky. He
couldn't be sure, but it was almost a perfect spot for an
ambush. He was out in the open though, and if he tipped
off whoever it was up there—if it was anyone—the bush-
whacker would have a much better shot than would he. He
halted the big stallion. Dismounting, he lifted the stallion's
left foreleg, looking under its belly toward the rocks. Again,
he thought he saw a slight movement.

He let the leg down and patted the horse and talked to
it. If anyone was up there, he wanted him to think that the
Appaloosa had gone lame, and he was tending it. Then he
pulled off the saddle and carried it off to the side of the
road. He went back to the horse, took the reins, and led it
off the road and back a little farther. If there was really

someone up there who was up to no good, Slocum wanted the horse to be out of danger, out of the line of fire. Moving back to the spot where he had dropped his saddle, he sat down and took a long drink of water out of his canteen. Out of the corner of his eye, he kept looking at the boulders. He capped the canteen and put it down. Then he took a cigar out of his pocket and stuck it in his mouth. He pulled out a match and struck it on a rock there on the ground, and he lit his cigar. He sat and puffed.

His Winchester was right there with the saddle within easy reach. He puffed and watched. For a while there was no discernible movement, and he began to think that he was just being jumpy, that there was really nothing there to worry about. Then he saw unmistakable motion, and then a rifle barrel was laid across a boulder. It was pointed at him. It was clear, and it was real. Slocum flattened himself on the ground behind his saddle just as a bullet thudded into the saddle. He reached for the Winchester, jerking it free of the scabbard. Rolling onto his back, he cranked a shell into the chamber. Another shot rang out from up on the boulders. This one kicked up dirt a couple of feet away. Slocum aimed at the spot where he could still see the rifle barrel, and he snapped off a shot. The rifle barrel disappeared as its shooter ducked.

Slocum got up to his feet and, ducking low, ran across to the right side of the road. Once across, he hit the ground and rolled, coming to a stop behind a clump of brush. A shot rang out and kicked up dust a few feet ahead of him. He took aim and sent a shot back in answer. The shooter ducked again. He was crawling around in those boulders, changing positions. Slocum got up and ran again. He ran toward the boulders and still to the right. He took a dive behind a high spot of ground. Another shot was fired from the boulders. It was wide to the left. Slocum fired back, got up, and ran again. He found a tree not far ahead and stopped behind it, standing, pressing himself against it. Peeking around the thick trunk, he saw a saddled horse. It had to belong to the shooter.

"Hey, you up there," he called out. There was no answer. "Can you hear me up there?" he called.

A rifle shot cracked for his answer. Whoever the son of a bitch was, he didn't want to talk. That was clear.

"How'd you like to be stuck out here afoot?" Slocum yelled.

Up in the rocks, Trump suddenly realized what Slocum was talking about. Slocum had worked his way into a position where he had a good view of Trump's horse—a good view and a good, clear shot. The son of a bitch could shoot the horse and run back to his own horse the way he made it to the position he was in. He had tricked him already into shooting before he was ready. Those first few shots had been long, too long. Now he was in a position to be threatening Trump's mount. In this country, that meant threatening his life.

"You wouldn't do that," Trump shouted. "You wouldn't shoot my horse, would you? That's a cruel thing to do."

"Is it worse than shooting a man?" Slocum called out. "You tried to shoot me. I don't even know who the hell you are."

Then Slocum raised his Winchester to his shoulder and took careful aim. He did not want to kill the horse, but he did want to frighten it, and more than that, he wanted to frighten the man. He squeezed the trigger and a bullet hit the ground a few feet away from the horse. The startled animal neighed, stamped, and ran. A shot from the rocks sounded and the lead thudded into the tree trunk behind which Slocum was secured. *A pretty good shot,* Slocum thought. *I'd best be careful with this one.*

"You son of a bitch," Trump yelled from the rocks. "You've run off my horse. You've stranded me out here."

"Yep. You're on foot for sure now, boy," Slocum yelled, "unless you can get through me to my horse. 'Course, they ain't many besides me who can ride that stallion. You might be stuck out here no matter what."

Trump fired again. "Yeah?" he shouted. "Well, you're stuck behind that tree, ain't you? You son of a bitch. How long can you stay there? Huh?"

"At least as long as you can stay up there on those rocks," Slocum answered. "It ought to be getting pretty hot up there about now. You take your canteen up there with you, or is it on your saddle?"

Trump's canteen was indeed with his saddle and so, gone with his horse, and his mouth and lips felt suddenly very dry. Desperate all of a sudden, he started inching his way to the far side of the boulders, hoping that Slocum would not detect his movements. He made his way down from them on the far side. Then standing on the ground, he started to work his way around to the side nearest the road. If his idea worked, Slocum would be watching the top and might not notice him peek around from the ground for his next shot. He made it, and he located the tree again. He still could not see Slocum, but he figured that if he stepped quickly out into the road, he would have the right angle to see the man on the other side of the tree trunk. He made the decision to try it.

Trump almost jumped into the center of the road, but he was astonished that he did not see Slocum behind the tree. Suddenly Slocum stood up from a new position off to the right of the tree. His rifle was ready for action.

"Call it off, boy," Slocum said. "You don't need to die here."

Trump swept the barrel of his rifle around to point at Slocum, and Slocum pulled the trigger. As Trump pulled his own trigger, he felt Slocum's rifle slug smash his chest. He cried out in pain and surprise and staggered back three steps. He lowered his rifle barrel slowly until it was pointed at the ground just a few feet in front of him. He strained as if he would raise it again. He wavered. Then he fell back hard.

Slocum, holding his rifle ready all the time, walked toward the fallen man. He was pretty sure the man was incapacitated, if not already dead, but he would take no foolish chances. He took his time, and he did not take his eyes off the man. Closer, he could see that the rifle had fallen where it was out of the man's reach. He walked even closer. He could hear Trump's gurgling breath. He stopped, still standing, and looked down into the man's face.

"I don't even know you," he said. "Why'd you make me do this?"

"One—One—"

The dying man was having trouble forming words, but Slocum figured him out. "One Shot?" he said. "Aaron Parsons. He put you up to this."

Trump nodded slightly. Slocum dropped to one knee. He felt in Trump's shirt pocket and found the one hundred dollars Parsons had give him. He held it in front of Trump's face.

"This what he paid you?" he asked.

Trump nodded again, weakly.

"Was it worth dying for?" Slocum asked. "You sold yourself too cheap, boy."

Trump stopped breathing, and his head rolled to one side. Slocum stood up, tucked the hundred into his own pocket, and turned to walk back to where he had left his horse. So One Shot had gotten this stupid young man killed just to delay him. In a way that was comforting. It meant that Parsons was not totally confident in his own abilities, at least not when it came to facing someone who had some experience in this area. Back where he had left his saddle and other things, he picked up the saddle and walked over to the big horse. He saddled up and packed up again, ready to get back on Parsons's trail. As he was about to ride past the body in the road, he stopped. He had not meant to, but he decided to at least bury the poor fellow. He thought that he would also catch up to the horse and free it of saddle and halter.

Harleyville was like a circus. Once Jimson had wired the governor's office, reporting on his progress in the matter of Parley Young, the governor had wasted no time in sending down a judge to hold a trial for the jailful of prisoners Jimson was holding. Judge Tally hit town and almost immediately began the trial. Charges were made and witnesses were called. No one, however, could come up with hard evidence that any of the prisoners had done any of the killings. At one point in the trial, when it looked like things might be getting just a little too hot for the prisoners, Orwig had voluntarily accused the dead Jerry Goodall of all the killings, including that of the former sheriff of Harleyville. He said further that he knew firsthand that Goodall had done the dirty deeds under direct orders from Parley Young. The judge at last ordered a recess. He needed time to think over all the evidence. At the appointed time, court was reconvened. Tally rapped on the bench with his gavel. The accused all stood to hear their fate. Tally glared at them in silence for a long moment. They all looked down and began to shuffle their feet nervously.

"Here's my ruling," Tally said at last. "It's final, and it's irrevocable. We all believe that these prisoners here had something to do with all the killings that have been going on down here, but we have no real evidence against any of them. We do have their own testimony that the killings were done by one Jerry Goodall, deceased, under orders from their boss, Parley Young. The court orders that warrants be sworn out for the arrest and apprehension of Parley Young on the charge of murder.

"Now as to these prisoners here, we find that there is insufficient evidence to pass sentence on them. However, there is strong and sufficient reason to suspect them of various nefarious deeds and to want them well out of this jurisdiction—permanently. Now listen to me, you prisoners at the bar of justice, and listen good. Here's my decision and my orders regarding your final disposition on the matters at hand. I'm turning you loose with orders to get the hell out of this country. Do you understand me real good?"

"Yes, Your Honor," said Orwig. "You sure don't have to worry none about that, sir. We'll all clear right out of here for sure. We'll all head straight on down for Texas. Maybe all the way down into Mexico."

"Either one of those places will be a hell of a lot better than here for you and for us," Tally said. He gave a hard rap with his gavel. "You can get on out of here right now. No sense in wasting time."

"Uh, Your Honor?" Orwig said.

"What is it?" Tally snapped.

"What about our guns?"

"What about them?" Tally said. "Where are they?"

"Ole Jimson made us dump them in a pile out there at Young's place when he went and arrested us," Orwig said. "I guess they're still out there. Going down there into that rough country south of here, a man had ought to be well armed, you know, for his own protection."

"Sounds to me like a pile out at Young's place is a good place for them," Tally said. "You get into any trouble, you'll have brought it all onto yourselves. Now, you'll be watched for a ways riding out of town, and if any of you ride in any direction but straight south, you'll be brought right back here and thrown back in jail. I'll come up with some charge that'll stick. Now get going."

As soon as the trial was adjourned, Jimson walked over to the judge's side. "Is what you just did really legal, Your Honor?" he asked in a low voice.

"Hell no," Tally said, "but if you repeat me on that, I'll throw your ass in jail. Good riddance to the bastards."

"I fully agree, Your Honor," Jimson said.

The lucky former gun hands of Parley Young left the courtroom, climbed on their horses, and headed out of town, riding south. Cheering Jimson, cowhands and other local folks mounted up and followed them out of town, jeering, taunting, and laughing. Orwig and the others had ridden south some miles before their tormentors stopped, turned, and rode back toward Harleyville. When he was sure that they were no longer being followed, Orwig stopped riding. The others stopped as well.

"Boys," Orwig said, "I ain't going to Texas."

"But you told the judge—"

"I know what I told that old son of a bitch," Orwig said, "but I ain't going. Hell, it's hotter for me in Texas than it is right here. I'm moving out offa the road and slip around to Young's place and get my guns. Then I'm riding north."

"But if they catch you—"

"I'll make a wide sweep around Harleyville," Orwig said. "You can be sure of that. Anyone going with me?"

There was a moment of silence. Then Snider said, "I'm going on down to Texas, like we said."

"See you boys around," Orwig said, and he turned his horse west and left the road. The others continued south. True to his word, Orwig made his way secretly back to the Young ranch, and he found the guns piled where they had been left. He found his own and swiped at it with his bandanna. Then he reholstered it and strapped the belt on around his waist. He mounted up and headed north.

Standing on the sidewalk back in Harleyville, Jimson put an arm around Molly. "Well," he said, "it's mostly over."

"I'll feel a whole lot better when Slocum and Buttermilk are back safe and sound," Molly said.

"You and me both," Jimson said. "It won't all be really over till then."

"I'm thinking about Felicia, too," Molly said. "The poor girl's been dealt some rough hands by fate. Buttermilk's probably the best thing that's happened for her in her life. I don't want to see anything go wrong. Carl?"

"What?"

"Where will they live after they're married?"

"I hadn't thought about that," he said. "Neither one of them's said anything to me about it, and I guess I've just been too busy with this other business to think about much of anything else."

"You know that line shack out on the east pasture?" Molly asked.

"Yeah," he said.

"It's good enough that it could be cleaned up and remodeled, don't you think?"

"By God, Molly," he said. "It sure could. I'll get some of the boys working on it right away."

"Wonderful," she said.

Thinking that he was far enough north of Harleyville, Orwig moved back down onto the road. It was easy going. He was riding along feeling sorry for himself and angry with Young for having abandoned him the way he had done. He didn't think too much about Parsons. After all, Parsons was just another hired hand. He noticed a couple of riders coming his way from the north, but he didn't think too much of that either, not until they were closer and he recognized Parley Young. Then he recognized Buttermilk as one of Jimson's crew. He thought about leaving the road, but he realized that they had seen him, too, so he just kept riding toward them casually.

When Buttermilk recognized Orwig, he stopped himself and Young and waited. Orwig rode up close and stopped. "You don't want to shoot it out," Buttermilk said. "Drop that gun."

"Wait a minute," Orwig said, raising his hands high. "I've done been put on trial back yonder and released. Insufficient evidence, the judge said. He told me to get out of the country, though, and I'm a getting."

"All I have is your word for that," Buttermilk said. "You'd better ride on back with me. If you ain't lying to me, I'll turn you loose again."

"Damn it, I ain't lying," Orwig said. "They do want that son of a bitch you're bringing in though. They want him for ordering all them killings."

"What do you mean by that?" Young said. "If there was insufficient evidence on you, how could there be any against me?"

" 'Cause I told them about you, you bastard," Orwig said. "After the way you went and run out on us, I was glad to. I just wish I could go back and watch you hang, but I been ordered out of the country."

"Take him back with us, Smith," Young said. "I can tell a few things on him, too, if that's his game. He's likely lying about that trial anyhow. There probably ain't been one. Arrest him and take him along with us."

"You bastard," said Orwig, and he reached for his six-gun. Buttermilk reacted quickly, but just as his slug tore into Orwig's chest, Orwig's bullet crashed into Young's forehead. Both men were dead when they hit the ground.

Buttermilk shoved back his hat and scratched his head.

"Well, I'll be damned," he said. He got off his horse, loaded the two bodies on their respective horses, tied them securely, and continued on his way to Harleyville.

18

Slocum hit another town a couple of days later after a lonely trail. He was moving farther and farther west, and he did not seem to be getting any closer to Parsons. In Singletree he followed his usual practice of stopping at the nearest saloon and giving the bartender a description of Parsons. The bartender in Singletree pretended ignorance. Slocum ordered a drink. It occurred to him that if he did not end this quest soon, he was going to be out of money. He did not notice the bartender whisper to another customer and the customer hustle out of the saloon. He drank his whiskey and ordered another.

At just about that time, a short, pot-bellied man of around forty, wearing a badge on a vest, walked into the saloon. He made straight for Slocum. Bellying up to the bar beside Slocum, he ordered himself a drink. Slocum noticed the closeness of the man, and he noticed the badge. He sensed trouble, although he had no idea what form it might take. There was plenty of room at the bar. There was no reason for the lawman to have parked himself so close. The lawman took a drink.

"Just ride into town?" he asked.

"That's right," said Slocum.

"What's your business here?" the lawman asked.

"Just passing through," Slocum said.

"You got the look of a gunfighter about you," the lawman said. "The smell of death is on you. You ain't just passing through. I asked you, what's your business here."

"And I told you," said Slocum. "Just passing through."

The lawman put down his empty glass and turned sideways to the bar so that he was facing Slocum. "Don't lie to me, boy," he said. "I heard that you come in here asking after a man."

"I did," said Slocum. "I didn't learn anything, so I'm passing on through. If I'd found the man here in town, then I might have some business here."

"What's your name?" the lawman asked.

"Slocum."

"You got a first name?"

"John."

"I ain't heard of you," the lawman said. "Maybe you've heard of me. Hinch Lawton's my name. I'm the sheriff in Singletree."

"Can't say that I have," Slocum said.

"Yeah?" said Lawton. He pulled out his revolver and poked it in Slocum's ribs. "Lay your Colt on the bar," he said. "And don't try no gunfighter tricks. I'll blow a hole in you soon as blink."

Slocum eased his revolver out of the holster and put it on the bar in front of himself, and Lawton reached over with his left hand and took it. He stuck it in his waistband at the small of his back.

"What's this all about, Lawton?" Slocum asked. "I just got in town. I haven't been here long enough to break any laws."

"Let's you and me take a walk over to the jailhouse," Lawton said. "Maybe I'll tell you over there."

Slocum lifted his glass and finished it. Then he turned and walked out the front door, Lawton following. On the sidewalk, Lawton said, "Turn right." Slocum turned and walked. In a short while he found himself in front of the jail. Lawton told him to go inside and Slocum did. Then

Lawton threw a cell door open wide. Slocum walked in. Lawton closed the door and locked it.

"Are you going to tell me what this is all about?" Slocum asked.

"I'm going to check through all my dodgers," Lawton said, "and if I don't find you on one of them, then I'm going to start sending out wires around the country with your name on them. I mean to find out if you're wanted anywhere. If you are, and I bet you are, then I'll damn sure find out. You can count on that."

"All you're doing is wasting my time," Slocum said. "I told you, I'm just passing through."

"Yeah," Lawton said, sitting down at his desk and pulling a stack of posters out of a drawer. "Just who is it you're supposed to be looking for anyhow?"

"I'm tracking a gunslinger name of Aaron Parsons," Slocum said. "They sometimes call him One Shot."

"Yeah. Yeah," Lawton said. "I heard of One Shot. What do you mean to do when you find him? Join up with him?"

"When I find him," said Slocum, "I mean to take him back with me to a town called Harleyville. If he won't go, then I mean to kill him."

"You're a goddamned bounty hunter," Lawton said. "Is there a price on this Parsons's head?"

"I don't know," said Slocum. "He's wanted in Harleyville. Actually, I'm a temporary deputy marshal. I just don't like to admit to it."

"Well, hell," Lawton said, tossing aside the stack of posters, "I don't see you in here. Just go on ahead and get comfortable, though. I'll be back."

"When you go to sending out those wires," Slocum said, "why don't you send the first one to Marshal Jimson at Harleyville?"

"Bullshit," Lawton said as he walked out the door. Slocum thought that he'd like to get the stupid son of a bitch outside of his little one-horse town face-to-face. He sat down on the cot to wait. There really was nothing that Lawton could do to him. He wasn't wanted for anything, and when Lawton made that discovery, he would have to turn him loose. The question was, how long would it take him to come to that decision. In the meantime, Parsons was getting farther and farther ahead.

It was maybe a half hour later when Lawton came back in holding a paper in his hands and studying it. He went to the back side of his desk and sat down. He put the paper down and studied it some more. At last he spoke. "Well," he said, "this Jimson does say that you're one of his deputies. I ain't sure though. I never heard of a Marshal Jimson. I got to check this out a little farther."

"Goddamn it," Slocum said, losing his patience, "Jimson got his commission just recently straight from the governor. He was commissioned to straighten out a mess down there at Harleyville, and when it's all taken care of, why, he'll just go back to being a private citizen again. He sent me out after Parsons. That's the whole story, except that you're interfering with a legal pursuit."

He thought about what he had just said, and he could hardly believe his own words. What's worse, he thought, they're all true. He sure would be glad to get this all over with. Lawton was scratching his head when a man with a green shade on his forehead came into the office. He went over to the desk and handed Lawton a paper. "This just came in for you," he said. "Looks like it might be important."

Lawton took it and began to read studiously as the man went back out of the office. "I'll be damned," he said. Shaking his head, he went for the keys on a hook on the wall, walked over to the cell, and unlocked it. "You're clear," he said. "Your gun's laying over there on my desk."

Slocum walked over to the desk, picked up his Colt, holstered it, then picked up the piece of paper that had just been delivered. It was a telegram, and it had come from the governor's office. It told Lawton in no-uncertain terms that Slocum was indeed a deputy of Marshal Jimson, that Jimson was indeed a marshal appointed by the governor, and that Lawton had damned well better stop interfering.

"Hey, that's private," Lawton said.

"If I had it in writing what a damned fool I was," Slocum said, "I'd want to keep it private, too."

He tossed the wire message back down on the desktop, fought off an urge to knock the shit out of Lawton, and walked outside. He was headed for his horse when Lawton stepped outside and yelled.

"Hey, Slocum," he said. "That man you're looking for—Parsons—he was here. Rode out of here early this morning. He's got better than half a day on you. He left out of here riding west."

Slocum paused and swallowed hard. "Thanks," he said.

Slocum rode west thinking about his little confrontation back there with Lawton. He had given the man the line about being a deputy marshal, and of course he had not lied. The only thing about it was that it was distasteful to Slocum. He had only allowed it in the first place because it had been convenient to Jimson, and he was helping Jimson out in his problem with Parley Young. He had used the line himself back there with Lawton for a similar reason. It had been convenient. He hoped he wouldn't have to do that again.

When Buttermilk rode into Harleyville with the two corpses, there was a major celebration in the streets. Buttermilk fought his way through the happy crowd and got himself into the office now occupied by Carl Jimson. Jimson greeted him with a warm hug. Buttermilk told Jimson about the encounter on the road and how the two men had gotten themselves killed. Then Jimson told Buttermilk about the trial in Harleyville.

"Well, I'll be damned," Buttermilk said. "Ole Orwig wasn't lying about that. The damn fool went and got himself killed for nothing."

"Looks that way, don't it?" Jimson said. "Well, that's the way his kind always wind up."

Buttermilk wondered if Jimson would think the same way about the Rock Port Kid, but then, he told himself that it didn't really matter. The Rock Port Kid no longer existed.

"Well, boy," Jimson said, "you did a good job. What about Slocum?"

Buttermilk heaved a sigh. "Far as I know," he said, "he's still out there on the trail of that damned Parsons. See, whenever Parsons and Young split up, well, so did me and ole Slocum. I went after Young, and Slocum, he went after Parsons."

"I got a wire from a small-town sheriff out west," said Jimson, "checking to make sure Slocum is really a deputy marshal."

"Sounds like he's all right then," Buttermilk said, "and he's still on the trail."

"Yeah," said Jimson. "Well, right now I believe that this place here can hold itself together without us. Let's you and me ride on out to the ranch. I got something out there I want to show you."

It was a long ride, and when they rode right past the ranch house, Buttermilk knew that something was up. Finally they reached the line shack that Molly had mentioned to Jimson. Several cowhands were at work on the outside of the building. They all greeted Buttermilk as he rode up with Jimson. Buttermilk gave Jimson a puzzled look.

"What's going on here?" he asked.

"Just what it looks like," Jimson said. "A little sprucing up. That's all. Why don't you climb down and take a look inside?"

Buttermilk swung down out of the saddle and walked over to the front door. He hesitated, almost as if he were afraid to go inside. "Go on," Jimson said. Buttermilk opened the door and stepped inside. His eyes opened wide and his jaw dropped. He saw Molly Jimson and Felicia at work measuring the windows for curtains. Felicia looked around and saw that it was Buttermilk who had come in the door. She smiled and rushed to his arms.

"Buttermilk," she said, "I'm so glad to see you."

"I'm tickled to see you, darlin'," he said, "but what in the world's going on here? I ain't never seen no line shack fancied up like this before."

"It's not a line shack," Felicia said, "not anymore. It's our home. Mr. and Mrs. Jimson have given it to us for our first home. Isn't it wonderful?"

"Well, gosh," Buttermilk said, "it sure is, but I don't know what to say. I—"

Molly decided to interject herself into the conversation just then. "Don't say anything, young man," she said, "just get on out there and help those boys with whatever it is they're doing on the outside. The sooner your place is ready, the sooner we can have the wedding."

"Yes, ma'am," Buttermilk said. He started to turn to go back outside, but Felicia grabbed him and gave him a long kiss full on the lips. When at last she let him go, his face was red for having partaken in that scene in the presence of Mrs. Jimson. He tipped his hat and got out as quickly and graciously as he could manage. But once outside, he had to stop and think. The Jimsons were sure being nice to him, well, to him and Felicia. They were wonderful folks. But he was thinking of what Jimson had said about Tallman and "his kind." Buttermilk thought that he just could not let Mr. Jimson continue going to all this trouble and expense not knowing who he really was.

But Felicia was so happy in there with Molly fixing up the little house. Buttermilk thought about Jimson finding out the truth and calling a halt to everything. Why, it would break Felicia's heart. Even so, he couldn't start their life together off on a lie. He decided that he would have to tell Jimson, and there was no time like the present. Carl Jimson had dismounted and was talking to one of the cowhands. Buttermilk walked over to join them.

"Mr. Jimson," he said, "I need to talk with you—in private."

"Well, sure, son," Jimson said. "Come on. Let's take a walk."

The two men strolled casually out of earshot of anyone else around. Then, when they had stopped walking, Buttermilk looked at the ground for a few seconds. Finally, he spoke.

"Boss," he said, "you're being real good to me and Felicia, and I surely do appreciate it, but there's something I got to tell you before this goes any further."

"All right, Buttermilk," Jimson said. "What is it?"

"Well, I don't know if you heard of the Rock Port Kid or not—"

"I have," said Jimson.

"Well, sir, I ain't really Buttermilk Smith. I'm the Rock Port Kid. I been living a lie here with you these last two years. I never meant to lie to you. I just wanted a clean start. That's all."

"Hmm," Jimson muttered. "I always heard that the Rock Port Kid was a real bad one. Killed a lot of men."

"He killed enough," Buttermilk said. "Too many, but it was all in that range war. It got him a hell of a reputation that he never wanted. That's how it come to him to decide to disappear like he done. That's when I come up here to you. That's the whole truth of it, Mr. Jimson, and now if you want me to leave, I will. You won't get no arguments out of me."

A stern expression settled on Jimson's face. "Buttermilk," he said.

"Yes sir?"

"This might surprise you, but I've known who you were all along."

"You have?" Buttermilk said, almost disbelieving.

"Sure I have," said Jimson. "Hell, you don't think the governor made me a marshal 'cause I'm stupid, do you?"

Jimson chose to lie to Buttermilk to cover up for Slocum's broken promise to keep Buttermilk's secret. It seemed like a good idea.

"Well, no sir," Buttermilk said. "I never thought that."

"As far as I'm concerned," Jimson said, "you're whoever you say you are. I believe that so-called Rock Port Kid is dead. Now, I suggest you go over there and pick up a hammer. If you pitch in and help, I think we can have this house finished in two more days. Then we can have us a wedding around here."

"Yes sir," Buttermilk said, and he turned and ran toward the other working cowhands.

•   •   •

Slocum was trail weary and so was the big Appaloosa. He'd lost track of how many days he had been on the trail of Parsons. There had been a couple more small towns along the way. The only thing he'd learned that he hadn't known before was that Parsons was riding a roan with a white stocking on its left foreleg. He knew that he was still on the right trail, though he was pretty sure that he was still a half day to a day behind, and he was determined to keep moving.

He had decided, though, that he was not going to hurry. He would plod along in the bastard's tracks, and sooner or later, Parsons would stop for more than a day. That would be when Slocum would catch up to him. And enough time had passed that ole One Shot was probably feeling pretty sure that Slocum was no longer after him.

The countryside was barren and boring, and Slocum was longing for another town. He had made up his mind that, Parsons or no, he was stopping for a bit of a rest at the next sign of civilization. A bath, a hot meal, a night's sleep in a bed, all that would be great. It was almost a necessity. And he was sure that the Appaloosa would feel just the same way about a stable and some good oats. The next town would be the place. He promised himself, and out loud, he promised the horse.

These were the thoughts that occupied his mind as he rode along. Of course, Parsons was always on his mind somewhere, but since he knew that he was still some distance behind his prey, he was not on constant alert. He rode easy. When he knew himself to be getting close to One Shot, that would be the time to start concentrating and staying constantly alert. That would come later. In the meantime, he'd go easy, and he'd stop for that well-deserved rest at the next town, whatever it might be.

He was thinking those thoughts when he noticed a sign beside the road not far ahead. There must be a town coming up soon, he thought. It would be none too soon. He rode a little faster, anxious to see what the sign would say. Closer, he made out the crude letters on the rough board.

STATE LINE

"Damn," he said out loud. His status as deputy marshal would not cross that line with him. Over there, he would be just what Sheriff Lawton had suspected him to be—a bounty hunter.

19

The next town was Shag's Crossing. It was built alongside
a river, and because of the river, the boring landscape had
changed. There were green trees lining the riverbanks. The
sight was a relief to tired, trail-weary eyes. The Appaloosa
even seemed to perk up at the sight and the smell. Slocum
became more alert, too, knowing that at each town there
was the possibility that Parsons had stopped for a spell. He
might be anywhere in the crowd. And Shag's Crossing was
the busiest of the towns Slocum had yet encountered on
this wretched trip.

Watching the men on the street, Slocum headed for the
livery stable. The first order of business was to see to it
that his horse was well taken care of. He was pleased to
discover that the stable was clean. The liveryman seemed
knowledgeable, but more important, he seemed to like
horses. The Appaloosa should be in good hands at this
place. Slocum paid the man in advance, instructing him to
give the horse all the best treatment. Then he started walking down the street, looking for a good hotel. He spotted
what looked like a good prospect about halfway down the
block and on the other side of the street. Then something
made him stop.

He stood and thought for a moment. Then he turned and walked back to the livery. He walked inside and stopped at the first stall. A roan stood behind the door. The liveryman came walking over. "Something more?" he asked. Slocum bent over to look under the door. There was the stocking on the foreleg. He straightened up again.

"No," he said. "No. I just wanted to look at this horse."

"I don't think it's for sale," the man said.

"Oh, that's all right," said Slocum. "I'm not really interested in buying it. I was just curious about that one stocking. That's all."

"Well, if you want to talk to the man," the liveryman said, "his name's Parsons. I think he's staying over at the Grange."

"Thanks," said Slocum, and he walked out of the livery again. *The Grange,* he thought. *That's the place I was headed for. Well, why not,* he decided. He walked down the street until he came to the Grange, and he went inside. He asked for a room and a bath. It would take a few minutes to get the hot water and have the bath ready, so he took his room key and went outside to look for a saloon. There was one right next door. Slocum went inside and bought himself a glass of whiskey. He stood at the bar to drink it. Taking advantage of the situation, he also looked over the crowd in the room, but he did not see Parsons. When he was done with his drink, he went back to the hotel and upstairs to his room. The bath was ready.

Slocum smoked a cigar while he soaked in his hot bath. When he finally decided to come out, he dried himself and dressed in clean clothes. Then he counted his money and went out to find a good steak. The place he found was across the street and down a few doors. It looked good, and he decided to take a chance. He was glad he did. The steak was delicious. He finished it and was about to get up to leave when Aaron Parsons came in. There was no mistake. Slocum stayed in his chair. The waiter came back around, and Slocum asked for another cup of coffee. He kept his eyes on Parsons.

Parsons found himself a table and sat down. It wasn't

long before he noticed Slocum watching him. At first it seemed as if he didn't really think that Slocum was deliberately staring at him. He looked away. Then he looked back, and Slocum was still staring. There was no mistake about it. Slocum wondered if the man had ever gotten a good look at him back in Harleyville. Maybe he didn't recognize him. No matter. The stare would accomplish the same purpose as if he had been recognized. The waiter stopped by Parsons's table and took his order. That distraction out of the way, Parsons looked back at Slocum and found him still staring.

Slocum calculated just about how long Parsons would take the stare, and just before he figured Parsons would lose his patience, Slocum got up and left the restaurant. He walked down the street until he found the local sheriff's office. Opening the door, he looked in. The sheriff was seated behind his desk. Slocum walked in, and the sheriff looked up.

"Something I can do for you, mister?" he asked.

"I want to give you some information," Slocum said.

"What's your name?" the sheriff asked.

"I'm John Slocum."

The sheriff stood up and offered his hand. "Slocum," he said, "I'm Taylor. What is it you want to tell me?"

"There's a man in town named Aaron Parsons," Slocum said.

"I know who he is," said Taylor. "I've been watching him. Far as I know, he's not wanted for anything. He's just got a bad reputation. What's your interest?"

"I been tracking him all the way from Harleyville," Slocum said. "He's wanted there. He came across the state line to get away from me, but I'm still after him. I mean to take him back with me or kill him. I just thought you'd like to know that I'm fixing to make some trouble in your town."

"You a lawman, Slocum?" the sheriff asked.

"Not by persuasion," Slocum said. "A rancher name of Jimson back there at Harleyville was good to me. He got into a range war with a man named Young. I decided to stick around and help. Jimson likes things done according to the law, though, so he went to the governor for help, but the governor gave him a marshal's commission, and then ole Jimson made all of his hands, me included, deputies. As soon as I take care of Parsons, I'll be resigning."

"So you are a lawman."

"Not over here," Slocum said. "But that ain't going to stop me."

"You made that clear," Taylor said. "Just don't do anything to make me have to come after you."

"I won't shoot him in the back," Slocum said.

"If it comes to shooting," Taylor said, "you just make sure that he goes for his gun first, and that there are plenty of witnesses around. But also make sure that no innocent bystanders get hurt. If you can manage it, I'd appreciate it if you take care of it outside of my jurisdiction. You know, I'm just a town sheriff."

"I'll do my best, Sheriff Taylor," Slocum said. "See you."

He left the sheriff's office and walked back to the hotel. He picked up a newspaper that was lying on a chair, took a seat in a comfortable overstuffed lounger, and started to read the paper. He had almost finished the paper when the thing he was waiting for happened. Parsons came walking into the lobby from outside. Slocum watched him over the top of the paper. He could tell that Parsons saw him, but ole One Shot seemed to try to ignore his presence there. Slocum's tactic was working. One Shot was getting nervous. He was wondering just who Slocum was and why he was watching his every move.

Of course, when Slocum began this game, he had no idea how Parsons would react. He might have gotten into a gunfight right away. Or Parsons might have confronted him verbally. But so far, neither of those possibilities had taken place. Slocum wondered how long the notorious gunfighter would put up with his annoyance. How soon would he run out of patience? And just what would he do? Parsons picked up the key to his room from the clerk at the desk and mounted the stairs. Slocum put aside the newspaper and left the building. He felt like having a drink.

He did not see One Shot again that evening, but early the next morning he planted himself again in the comfortable chair in the hotel lobby. Again he picked up a newspaper and waited. In a while, Parsons came down the stairs. When he saw Slocum sitting there, he hesitated. He looked at Slocum. Slocum looked at him over the newspaper, and he felt almost sure that One Shot would say something. The gunfighter did not. Instead he turned around and went back upstairs. Slocum waited. It wasn't long before Parsons came back down carrying his saddlebags and his bedroll. He stopped at the desk and paid his bill. Then he left.

Slocum waited a moment, put down the newspaper, and stepped outside. Leaning against the outside front wall of the hotel, he lit a cigar and watched Parsons walk down the street. Parsons went straight to the livery stable. Slocum kept watching. In a few minutes, Parsons came back out, leading his saddled horse. He climbed up onto the animal's back and started riding. He left town headed west. Slocum went back into the hotel. In a few more minutes, he was again on the trail of Parsons, but this time he knew that he was only a few minutes behind the man.

This time, Slocum rode hard. He knew that his big Appaloosa could catch the roan, even if Parsons was riding hard. A few miles out of town, a ridge ran alongside the left side of the road. Slocum veered off and rode up onto the ridge. It wasn't long after that he caught up with Parsons. Parsons heard the hoofbeats above and looked up to see Slocum riding there. He kicked his roan in the sides and began to run a race with the rider on the ridge, but the roan was no match for the Appaloosa. Soon Slocum was well ahead.

Down on the road, Parsons slowed his pace again. He moved on apprehensively, knowing that Slocum was somewhere ahead. The road made a curve to the left not far ahead, and from around the curve Parsons could see a wisp of smoke rising. Nervous and curious, he moved slowly on until he rounded the curve. There ahead, just off the north side of the road, Slocum sat beside a small fire. Parsons rode on up close. He started to speak, but Slocum beat him to it.

"Come on down and join me," he said. "I've got coffee making. You didn't have yours this morning."

Parsons swung down out of the saddle and cautiously approached Slocum's fire. He sat down directly across from Slocum while Slocum poured a cup of coffee, then handed it to him across the fire. Parsons sipped at it, eyeing Slocum all the while. Slocum picked up his own cup and drank.

"What's this all about?" Parsons said.

"You've been a hard man to catch," said Slocum.

"How long have you been on my trail?" asked Parsons.

"Since you left Harleyville," Slocum said.

"You a lawman?"

"Sort of," Slocum said.

"What's that mean?"

"You don't know?" Slocum asked.

"No," Parsons said. "Should I?"

"I was working for Carl Jimson," said Slocum. "Then Jimson went and got himself made into a marshal. He deputized all his hands. Me, too. So I'm Marshal Jimson's deputy. But you don't need to worry about that, 'cause I'm outside of our jurisdiction."

Parsons sipped some more coffee.

"I don't get it," he said. "If we're outside your jurisdiction, what's this all about?"

"You want some breakfast?" Slocum asked.

"I want to know what the hell this is all about," Parsons said.

"Let's eat first," Slocum said. He took out some cooking utensils, and he cooked beans, potatoes, and eggs. Then he dished them out on two plates and handed one to Parsons. "More coffee?" he asked. Parsons held out his cup, and Slocum poured it full. Then the two men ate in silence. When they were finished, Slocum refilled the cups. He took out two cigars and offered one to Parsons. They sat and smoked in silence for a moment.

"You followed me out of Harleyville to arrest me and take me back," Parsons said.

"That's right," Slocum admitted.

"But now you're out of your jurisdiction."

"Yeah." Slocum blew a cloud of blue smoke into the air and watched it float away.

"How come you didn't stop and go back when you come to the borderline?" Parsons asked.

"Oh, I can't arrest you over here," Slocum said, "but I still wanted to catch up with you."

"What for?"

"I want to ask you to ride back to Harleyville with me," Slocum said.

Parsons puffed at his cigar nervously. "You must be crazy," he said.

"Could be."

"I ain't going back there."

"Then I'll just have to kill you," said Slocum.

"You can try," Parsons said. "Do you know who I am?"

"Aaron Parsons," Slocum said. "They call you One Shot."

"And you think you can take me?"

"I think I'm older than you," Slocum said. "I've been at it longer than you have, and I'm still alive."

"I hate to waste a good smoke," Parsons said.

"Let's finish these cigars then," Slocum said.

"All right."

"You know," said Slocum, "you can still ride back with me."

"Not a chance," said Parsons.

"You want some more coffee?" Slocum asked.

"Sure," said Parsons. "After all, it might be my last cup—or yours."

Slocum picked up the pot and poured two more cups. "Yeah," he said. "It could be."

They sat like that across the fire from one another, sipping hot coffee and smoking cigars, and there was no more conversation. At last, his cup empty and his cigar a short butt, Slocum held up the butt and looked at it. Then he dropped it into the fire. Parsons picked up his cup and drank the last of his coffee. He took a final puff on his short cigar and tossed it into the fire. Both men stood up. Both men began backing away from one another. They stopped and stood still.

"Drop your gun belt and ride back with me," Slocum said.

"Thanks for your hospitality," said Parsons. He went for his gun, and it was out and firing in a flash. Slocum tossed himself to the side, but even so, he felt the sting of the bullet across the upper part of his left arm, just below the shoulder. He hit the ground and rolled, pulling his Colt at the same time. Another bullet kicked up dirt just where he had been. Still rolling, he raised the Colt and fired. His bullet crashed into One Shot's chest.

One Shot looked stunned, unbelieving. He tilted his head to look at the dark stain against the black of his shirt. His left hand moved up to feel the hot sticky liquid that was spewing forth from the hole in his chest. His legs wobbled, and he staggered back a couple of steps. His right arm sagged, and his fingers went limp. He dropped his revolver. Then he fell to his knees. He looked up at Slocum, and he opened his mouth as if he were about to say something. Then his eyes glazed over and he pitched forward on his face. He did not move again.

When Slocum rode into Harleyville, he was pleased to see horses tied to the rail in front of the sheriff's office. He rode his Appaloosa up to the rail and tied it there with them. Then he walked into the office. Carl Jimson popped up out of his chair and walked around the desk to take Slocum's hand and pump it vigorously.

"Damn, I'm glad to see you back," he said, "And just what is it you got there?"

Slocum tossed the flat-brimmed black hat onto the desk. Then he pulled the black leather gun belt off his shoulder and tossed it over beside the hat.

"It would've been a real unpleasant ride back," he said, "if I'd tried to bring back any more of him than that."

Jimson gave Slocum a serious look. "It's done then?" he said.

"I asked him to come back here with me " Slocum said. "He wouldn't have any of it, so we had to do it the hard way. He's dead all right. How about Buttermilk and Young?"

"Buttermilk got Young," Jimson said, "and he's back safe and sound. Married up with Felicia."

"I'm glad of that," Slocum said. "Does that mean I can quit this deputy job?"

"Yeah," Jimson said, "you can. And I want to tell you how much I appreciate what you've done for us here."

"Forget it," Slocum said. "You took me in when I needed help."

"You know," Jimson said, "you can stick around here as long as you like. Harleyville's going to need a new sheriff. I'll be asking the governor to relieve me of marshal's responsibilities now that the whole Young pack has been wiped out."

"Thank you, Mr. Jimson," said Slocum, "but I wasn't cut out to be a lawman. Wasn't even cut out to settle down at one job or stay in one place for very long. I think I'll be hitting the trail after I've had time to rest up a bit."

"Well then," Jimson said, "at least, you'll rest up out at the ranch. Buttermilk and Felicia will want to see you. Molly, too, and all of the boys. They'd never forgive me if I was to just let you ride off from here without so much as a so long."

"I'll take you up on that," said Slocum.

"In that case," Jimson said, "let's you and me walk over to the Red Ass and have us a glass of good whiskey. Then we'll ride out to the ranch and let everyone out there in on the good news."

Explore the exciting Old West with one of the men who made it wild!